THE CAUTIOUS HEART

*

A young man falls in love. Of the thousand faces
that pass by the piano which he plays in a small
London club, this one face contains his future.
Why? he says to himself—as, although in love, or
because he is in love, he questions the reasons that
make us fall for one, rather than the other person
whom in our lives we chance to meet.

Nor does this affair run easily. The story in-
volves a triangle of an unusual kind—where the
other man is not after the girl nor she after him.
He is instead an attachment, an old friend continu-
ally in trouble. These troubles become obsessional
with the girl Marie—and consequently with the
narrator, who has thus to share his love with a
shadow.

By the same Author
*
Novels
THE LOVING EYE
A BED OF ROSES
THE FACE OF INNOCENCE
THE BODY

Collected Short Stories
AMONG THE DAHLIAS
A CONTEST OF LADIES
LORD LOVE US
A TOUCH OF THE SUN
THE PASSIONATE NORTH
SOUTH
SOMETHING TERRIBLE
SOMETHING LOVELY
FIREMAN FLOWER

Short Novels
THREE
THE EQUILIBRIAD

Essays
PLEASURES STRANGE AND SIMPLE

Travel
THE ICICLE AND THE SUN

Miscellaneous
WESTMINSTER IN WAR

Children's Stories
IT WAS REALLY CHARLIE'S CASTLE
THE LIGHT THAT WENT OUT

THE
CAUTIOUS
HEART

A Novel by

William Sansom

1958

THE HOGARTH PRESS

LONDON

Published by
The Hogarth Press Ltd.
42 William IV Street
London, W.C.2

*

Clarke, Irwin & Co. Ltd.
Toronto

02382422

Printed in Great Britain

© William Sansom 1958

I

'LOIS? This is Belle! I simply *had* to ring.

These words fell on a moment's silence in the murmurous bar, Belle pressed the button, coins dropped in the telephone box, and my life was changed forever.

She might as well have been pressing a button on my own body, say the nipple placed nearest the heart. Because in reply to her words, from a table somewhere behind me, there rose a voice I had never heard before but was soon to know too well. It was a man's voice, loud, delighted, and chanting like a lamp-post drunk:

'Ding dong Belle,' it sang, 'Pussy's in the—'

Then a whisper as someone, a woman, tried to quieten him.

A moment before, and for an hour before that, I had been contemplating the problem of boredom: or of ennui. Or of whatever one calls the dishwater mood, hopeless, enervated or over-nervous, which from time to time wraps its wet grey cloth across the beaming of our precious sunlight.

It seems to come in cycles; though irregularly. It is nothing as elevating as melancholy, nor as precious as ennui, nor as grave as world-weariness. It is a dull thing, like constipation, which may well be one of its causes. It is plain, stupid, reasonless boredom and nothing to be proud of.

Consider my own position that evening in the New Marlven Club. Around me rise discreet damask red walls dotted with old-gold fleurs-de-lys, some of which have fallen away to leave blank spaces of absorbing interest. More old-gold on the parchment-shaded wall-lamps, whose electric candles point askew from renaissance brackets. All around, on our thick-piled carpet alive with creeping Indian carrot-shapes, stand small refectory tables, carved and terribly cellulosed. Against one wall there lurches a great sheep-dog of a settee shaggy with giant fringes. And at the far end of the room rises the bar—a cynosure of gleaming oak with chromium trimmings, bright with bottles and glass and lit like an altar: behind this, Andrew the barboy officiates like a white-coated priest, his brilliantined hair haloed by miraculous, concealed lighting from above.

Opposite the settee my three-legged beast, my piano, sage-green and gold and battered, sidles against a wall that displays occasional hunting prints. Here it is that I am hired to play a little light jazz on Wednesday and Saturday evenings.

A room well-known to me, then, and rich with many another up-to-date curio, including a rollicking oil of cardinals in their cups, with a light above it, but with which we must not become dazzled at this first glance.

6

The Marlven indeed! One can imagine the nice tones with which this name was first suggested. 'Something classy!' And then the secretary spelling it wrong, and nobody bothering to correct it, and the printer and the sign-painter going straight ahead until, faced with an impasse, they, the Management—Belle and a retired Major and a Cypriot restaurateur—all agree that it is really rather good, something *new* about it. Ringing the changes. New, but old too. Risky but safe: which about describes the whole atmosphere of the place.

So here I am sitting in the New Marlven on a non-playing Tuesday, and bored, bored, bored. And bored with myself for being bored.

Boredom is one of the big sins, base, irresponsible, insensitive. When one thinks of all the fashionable exquisites who have made a virtue of such insensitivity! And why am I bored? I am provident. I am well. I have a number of interests—music, gramophone records; and I like pictures (even the kind that do not move). And I read (books, and I don't mean magazines). On another day, I would feel there is not time in all the world to do all the things I want to do: I would feel pressed for time—regretfully closing a book to fit in an exhibition before coming home to work through an orchestration or prepare for a recording session: impatient with time, still much like a child resenting the few precious minutes lost in having to brush his hair or go to the lavatory.

Yet today—nothing will do. These are the days when local shops and streets look used and known and lifeless—the same whose every appearance on another day would give pleasure: the days when one seems to see right into people, knowing everything about them, turning away without further interest, blind to all humours and tragedy and what at other times may seem miraculous, the beautiful persistence of living.

But today I can find nothing worth while and nothing to do and can scarcely bear to imagine how the next hours must drag by before it is decently time to think of bed, writing the dull day off . . . and then this ding-dong startles the room and I turn to see where it comes from, thinking no more than: 'Another drunk.'

A small dark woman in a dull brown dress and hat still tries to quieten the man with whom she sits, and who delightedly prolongs his little song.

He waggles a finger at her, giggling. He is at the still fairly sober stage when a drinker imitates, with impatient love, a drunk.

At the other end of the room Belle still grates on into the telephone '. . . and Elsie said don't get it, she said, fox or no fox those little glass eyes on your shoulder they'll send you nuts . . .'

And then this small woman happens to look up and meet my eye and, opening her teeth in a little nervous smile, raises her eyes to the ceiling in mock despair.

And I find myself smiling back. A number of things

suddenly grow and sprout all round and inside me. At this slight contact with an unknown dark brown woman, life comes flowing back.

I had seen her come in and had paid no attention. She was simply a pleasant-looking woman, composed and inheld and unsparkling. She and her moustached man, nonentitous in an ordinary suit, had sat down quietly in the dark light of those parchment lamps and neither had thrown out presence or personality, they had about them the settled and sparkless quiet that one may feel from a brother and sister passing the time together.

But now life flows in and details bud into place. One flicker of interest—and everything becomes significant. The man is definitely goodlooking—though he has a little of that monkeyish look given by a square military scrub of a moustache. His dark hair is plastered back straight with a careful parting. He has a squarish face and a strong button of a nose, his eyes glitter under thick eyebrows and overall there is about him the clipped clean-jawed hard-bitten look of a British officer from the Kaiser's War. Yet—looking more closely—he could not have been more than thirty or thirty-five years old! He is out of his time. He has probably modelled himself on his father, or some uncle—a common enough phenomenon. There is always this bewildering minority of people walking about out of time.

Just now he is a bit the better for drink, and hugely

amused with himself. His teeth show a glitter of gold, he waggles his short finger at the woman with the awkward indelicacy of a man used more to work than to gesture with his hands: and with his other arm he waves to Andrew the Bar for more drinks, which Andrew, wondering if he should, pours and brings to them.

The woman, after her brief smile at me, has returned her interest to him—and now laughs too, shrugging her shoulders in a kind of amused despair. She is not at all the dull brown shadow I had first imagined. First, this brown of her dress gleams subtle and rich as silken cherry-bark. And her skin shades into another kind of light brown or buff, a pale tea-brown from which deep rich sea-blue eyes glitter between thick black lashes. Hair black, red-black: and her features shaped and pointed—as people look like animals, she has the mouse look, a walnut of a mouse with a straight-up way of sitting; a gold thing hangs round her neck and brightens up all this quiet rich brownness. It is she, I notice with a fine flush of conventional resentment, who pays for the drinks.

And then Mr. and Mrs. Armitage come in, accompanied by the Adrians, Otto and Myra. They surround me in a little semi-circle smiling and asking me to get up and play some new tune then popular. I have to smile and say it is not my playing night, which means nothing to them, for they have no idea of the physical effort it takes to play that machine, quite apart from the repetitive boredom of it. But there—sometimes I would play a little and with joy on an offnight, and how were they to know? Nevertheless, the answer now is that 'I do not feel like it' and they feel I do not feel like discomposing myself for *them*. But this is a usual trouble—like dealing with those who always want *Tiger Rag*, which only makes you sweat and upsets everyone else, it's so noisy and fast. And like fobbing off the drunks who insist on some special sentimentality of theirs played slap in the middle of what you are already playing—yet these must be treated carefully, they are the most likely to give you a drink; when the master-maestro relationship becomes articulate in the phrase 'have a drink', spoken like an order. And if you are sitting up at the keys for a four-hour stretch, you are pleased to obey.

However, the point is that during all this time with the Armitages and Adrians I am prevented from looking over again to the table with that so suddenly appealing little brown mouse-woman, for the circle of suits and dresses and faces keeps it hidden. Armitage is a man 'in business'—a company director, and the company might be interested in anything from a slice in a block of flats to an espresso ring, from launderettes to car-hire. Tall, fifty, flashy, silver-haired, too pink and white to look quite healthy yet also spare and aquiline, like a big predatory check-suited bird. And Mrs. Armitage is a stout, blonde woman with a baby chicken's face and a tiny voice like a girl to match it.

These two birds talk endlessly to each other at a conspiratorial corner table more or less labelled with their name. Plainly affluent, one has wondered why they should come to such a place as the New Marlven at all—except that possibly this is one of the simple economies that might produce their affluence; or that, as with so many others of our members, it is simply the nearest place where a lady can be brought to drink, for the one homogeneous quality of the members of the New Marlven is that they do not like public houses.

The two charming soft small Adrians are also among the regulars. Otto with his dark eyes and grey hair and controlled plumpness stands five foot four in his smooth silk socks, and wife Myra, with her long nose and close eyes and perpetual melon of a smile, smiles up to him from an inch beneath. He is in the button business, she in some general export-import line—sugared fruits from the Levant, currants, delights. A childless couple, they have grown closer together for it, and now, in their forties, behave like young sweethearts. Charming and attentive to each other, a more generally kind and considerate pair one has never met—and their good pleasure in each other extends to a general enchantment with life. And with 'things'. They love jewellery and their fine soft clothes. One imagines them taking out expensive sets of pigskin luggage and playing with these late at night in their neat small sixth-floor flat. And the pleasure they would take in parcels arriving—cellophane, ribbon and smart cardboard boxes all over that expensive little flat. Yet they are neither excessively fashionable nor vulgar in these pretensions: they do not boast of possession but instead fondle all these things in the way a diamond merchant loves as much as assesses his diamonds; they love all things too much to be possessive of one or two.

And now, quite casually, beneath Otto's smile and framed in a triangle of dove-grey made by his soft-suited arm, a peculiar drama reveals itself. The protagonist is a human hand, some two tables away. Framed thus in Otto's suiting it seems to move independently of a body. Walking on its fingers along the tabletop like a pale white crab, it goes carefully towards a silver pepper-pot, hesitates at meeting it, sniffs at it with a forefinger—and then, quiet as a creature deep in water, pounces three fingers on it and slides it out of sight into the belly of the hand. A pause. Then slowly it retreats across the table and out of sight behind the edge of Otto's arm.

This is surely not the way to pick up a pepper-pot?

I move my head to one side to see where the hand has gone to—just in time to see it slip down off the table and scuttle into the side pocket of a man's blue suit. Had this little episode not been so acutely framed, I doubt whether I would have seen it at all. As it was, it loomed up too alertly, like something seen behind one in a mirror; and I poked my head right round Otto to see who it was—our new ding-a-dong customer sitting like a handsome officer in a blue suit with a hand in his pocket.

Does one act in such a matter? And if so—at what point? If you see a barman stealing a few shillings from a till, do you say: 'It's no business of mine,' assuring yourself that this kind of thing, anyhow, goes on all the time? Or do you tell the management? Do you act on principle, exposing yourself not only to all the long argument that must follow but probably also to the pitying smiles of all concerned, both sides, for being an interfering idiot, a funless informer?

In a very vague sense, I was part of the staff at the New Marlven. And I liked Belle, who was more or less the Management. But really . . . what can one do? The fellow was probably a souvenir grabber—one of those who collect enamel admonitions Not to Spit in Italian to place above their chimney-pieces. So—half-tipsy and having his fun? And yet . . . there had been something efficient and nearly professional about the way it had been done. Kleptomania then? Petty thieving?

I looked round the room, wondering still what one ought to do. The Armitages and Adrians had passed on to the bar. Andrew was serving them. Belle was talking to a couple of young men by the fruit machine. A television screen jigged bluely in another corner, a lonely man propped square on a stool opposite, staring it out, eating it. Few people about, nine on a Monday night—and thus easy enough for me to walk across to Belle and speak quietly to her. But then—kleptomania is a disease, and to be pitied? Petty pilfering goes on everywhere and in one way, heigh-ho, may be a useful sublimation of greater dishonesty? And all that . . . and putting it off I rose and walked over not to Belle but past the questionable table itself—with the idea of glancing down to see whether one or two other club oddments were still there, a silver olive fork and a little tray for chips.

As I passed the whole thing was decided. In the first place, no fork and chip-tray, both gone; and in the second place just then the man rose to his feet and fell over.

He lurched up with one arm waving—probably at the bar—and sat back suddenly half off his chair and then completely off and sprawled over the woman. The last drink must have done the trick. The whole table swayed—but not a glass fell and I found one indeed saved in my left hand, while my right grabbed his shoulder and pulled him upright.

'Whoops,' he said, smiling up at me. 'Thanks, old saviour.'

'Colin!' the woman says.

'Now you *have* had enough,' she says, smoothing herself down and glancing up at me and shaking her head at him all at the same time. 'Come on, we're off.'

And I say quietly: 'The night air'll hit him—can I help?'

She nods. Instantly sensible, accepting; yet composed

and independent. It is an immediate and strong impression, this independence.

It proves surprisingly easy to get him to the door. He stumbles a little; but he agrees. None of the usual drunk's repetitive nonsense. No childish hatred of leaving the party. No righteous anger at being thought drunk.

'You know,' he leers at me—and with my arm round his waist I feel we are really great old friends —'you know, this is *impossibly* good of you, old fellow. Isn't it good of him, Marie?' And he lolls his face round at her and she smiles her deep blue eyes at me, nodding yes, but never at all embarrassed.

'No trouble at all,' I say, pumping his arm into an overcoat that flaps suddenly alive, while she knots his scarf and he struggles deep in a pocket for change.

Outside in the street a few snowflakes are falling. The slow drift of white feathers across a street lantern warms the winter air. A car whirrs up and disappears into the gloom. A bus growls somewhere. The little light of a taxi shows far off.

'Home,' she says, turning us all to the left. 'It's not far,' she nods to me, 'first left, second right.'

So they live near! I too, but in the opposite direction. I had never seen them before: London neighbours by the length of a long village street, but far apart by the habit of a few turned corners.

So along familiar pavements washed clean of people by the night we walked him, stumbling rather more in the cold clear air. A neon sign glowed square and steady. I heard her say: 'It'll be nice to get to bed, won't it, Colin?'

'Hit the hay,' he nodded, very serious.

His feet lapsed sideways, and we all three seemed to traverse the pavement like a chorus line, and laughed —but through it I remember a sore little jolt of envy. The two together? I alone left out?

'I haven't seen you in the Marlven before,' I said, making talk. 'You don't go often?'

Her glove made a little circular gesture—her glove, was there a ring on the finger? 'I just became a member a night or two ago. I know you, though. You play.'

Her face shone like a lovely curved nut laid in fur against the falling flakes, her teeth smiled appreciation, simply a smiling definition that this was so, that I played: none of the usual flattery and wonder.

So we had already spent an evening in the same room together, and I had never known! Does this happen all the time—people perhaps even meeting, dancing, forgetting, then meeting again in a more acceptive mood finally to discover themselves?

'Awful dump,' Colin said, 'but she can't stand closed doors, Marie, can you? Must poke her nose in. Give me a pub any day.'

'When you live near,' she said. 'I like to know everything about where I live.'

Another side-step, slithering on the puddling brown snow. 'You've not been here long, then?'

'A year,' she said. 'It all takes time. Here we are.'

A brown street. Small railinged Early-Victorian houses, snowflakes falling white against dull cream facings. Three bells on the door, and all under a street lantern. Colin was plunging about in his pocket for a key, swaying a bit, but the better for a walk. I remember feeling far too deeply upset that here under this lamp I would be left alone, the door shut—and probably shut before I turned away. A bus off in Baker Street echoed its grinding gears, a sad and lonely sound on the quiet night air.

They began to thank me. He found the key. And then she said to him: 'You'll be all right now? I do wish you'd eat something?'

'Straight to bed,' he said. 'That's where I belong. Good night, Marie dear . . . you've been awfully good, both been good.'

And as the door closed on him and we two were left and my whole spirit went bounding absurdly high, she said in a flat voice: 'He simply won't eat.'

'And you?'

But she would neither have dinner, nor drink a cup of coffee. 'Let's walk a bit,' she said, 'I like this filthy weather.'

So we walked, and I thought: Here's a deep one. Because there is this thing about girls who walk at night and don't complain of the cold. Brooders. A bit strange in a nice way.

'And I thought he was your husband,' I laughed,

noticing that she did not. A slight shadow came across her face:

'Oh?'

'Or your fiancé or something,' I said to ease it.

'No. *He* isn't my fiancé.'

'Oh.'

Who was?

We turned another corner, and for a moment in that white and softly falling night faced the sharp freshness of a wind.

She buried her face down in fur against it, and my nose began to water—there was a breezy quayside feeling about, all the smell of wet winter at once, our feet padding in slush that tried to be white but melted at a touch to lamplit sepia.

'Who *is* your fiancé then?'

'An odd question,' she said, 'since you don't know who I am in the first place. In any case,' she added, '*was* my fiancé.'

'Was, then.'

'Why do you ask?'

'It's interesting. I mean, I'm interested.'

'How could it matter?' she said. I was watching her sideways for the shadow of regret. None came.

'It was—well, call it somebody. No bones, hearts broken. We spent a lot of time together, and one day I suddenly woke up to the fact that nothing would really ever be different, that this would go on and on, just as we were, whatever difference marriage made it

19

would really be the same, him, me, day after day—
and that felt dull, very dull indeed. Which could
hardly be right. So I broke it off, you know. He made
a polite enough fuss. and that's all there was to it. My,
I'm talking.'

This shadow man, although rejected, gave her life
a presence. There she was, she had had a life.

'I suppose it's because we haven't been introduced,'
she said.

'Pardon?'

A smell of cooking, of frying chops, rose meatily
from area railings.

'This intimate kind of talk. One talks to an absolute
stranger. You're wearing a confession box, you know?'

'It's a trifle tight on the shoulders.'

Well, everybody has a life. But now hers rose big
as a hotel vestibule, busy with apprehensions, hollow
as a stomach. She had seemed to confer an intimacy
a moment before, but she had spoken it drily, without
emotion. She was giving none of herself away. I only
knew that this had happened, this life; that her small
body primping about with short steps and with a cool
secret head on top of it had already had a life.

And I, walking the winter night streets with her—
what was I after? A simple young wolf on his sex-
prowl? Possibly—to begin with. But by now I was
involved in a much deeper matter, in a mystery of
personality—a strong and a self-contained one: and
such continence as hers is an immediate challenge to

instincts far wider than those of sex. It challenges the will to impress oneself: or what is loosely called the will to 'power', the will to make one's mark. But at the time, of course, I simply felt over-excited, and grateful —for walking beside her I was filled with an approximation of hero-worship, I was grateful to be allowed into the company of this enclosed brown mouse, to whom, looking down at her well beneath my shoulder, I looked up.

Yet what particularly was she? A woman met in a 'club' and called Marie. Not more than that? I knew she gestured with a small circle of the left hand, that there was a bracelet on her wrist, that her small feet pointed outwards as she walked, sparrowing the mouse. And so on. Physics. Why, then, not the next girl?

Self-congratulation and a mighty fine feeling for everyone, I tried to reflect, follows the gift of a helping hand. I was pleased with myself, V.C.

Nevertheless, I hung with a disproportionate interest on any words she had to say about herself. As we walked on—past railings, porticoes, steps, shops, placards, and then up another street with all these things over again—I learned that she lived in a top-floor flat alone, that her mother had died two years ago, and that she had scarcely known her father who had been killed when she was a child.

'He was a turk,' she said. And there were seconds of ambiguity before I saw that the word needed a capital, he was a Turk, which might account for the light touch of brown to her skin.

And they had lived in a top-heavy family house in Belsize Park. I heard about the pear-tree, the Victorian stained glass lights, the wet basement full of hide-and-seek cupboards and cellars. And her father had been an importer of Levantine spices and fruits.

Coincidence! Did she know the Adrians? My spirits rose, I who despise superstition thrummed with portent! But no, she didn't know them. This seemed to make no difference—big letters of augury blazed across my sky.

And she? She worked in Holborn. I had never known that Holborn had such hidden magic. She worked every day in an office, in a small investment trust company's office, as a kind of superior secretary —well, almost an executive, but *ex officio*. The way, she said, women do the work but don't get the position. When she said 'office' I smelled immediately the excitement of feminine odours among box-files, saw bare arms against a dust of documents, imagined the sprawl of nyloned legs beneath a typewriter—all those breaths of femininity that can exorcise, in one terrible excitant flash, the wood-aged maleness of offices.

And what was she noticing as we walked? She laughed at a cat with a white face and a misplaced moustache like an early film comedian's. She went silent after we passed an old woman wrapped up in newspaper on a doorstep. She made one bad bright joke—something about a musical conductor called Uncle Andante who lived at Nice. I forget how the nephew came in, but it was considerate of her, trying to please the musician in me.

Then I happened to mention Colin. For a moment she said nothing, and the sound of our shoes sloshed louder. Then: 'He's impossible,' she said, 'he's his own worst enemy. Poor Colin,' she sighed, winding herself up, and I could hear the breath she took to feed what now came like a cannonade of words, all constraint gone, 'you see, he's really quite brilliant, I wouldn't say a genius but talent, oh, yes, he's brimming with talent, you don't know he paints of course, that is he draws and designs, or did, because he's given that up to photograph, yes to photograph and the kind of thing he does is to hock his camera for the sake of a few drinks and there you have a common enough damned stupid situation, a photographer without a camera, and all for very little reason, which is so unreasonable, because when I said a few drinks I don't mean he's alcoholic it's just that he gives up, he's weak and irresponsible, he makes an effort and gets straight and then poof he blows it all to pieces, I mean whatever he's settled to, it's lunatic.'

She must have taken another breath, but there was hardly a pause: 'Of course he's had money, that's one of the troubles. Always had it, not always a lot but always some, and now when it's gone he thinks he somehow deserves it. I don't know, if only he'd settle and *do* something about it. There's something childish in people like him. He could do wonders if he tried. I hate waste. His father was a wine merchant, richish —he had all the schooling and everything. But the old man's dead and the business is bust. His mother helps him sometimes. His *mother*—at his age! Here we are.'

Above us rose an immense six-storey house built in a Dutch manner of red brick with yellow porcelain facings. It was a solid mansion. The stone steps were sharp as iron. A good deal of brass and many bell-buttons glittered from a heavy porch through which one could see a vestibule, an outer hall and an inner hall, and the iron cage of an old-fashioned lift.

'Have you known him long then?' I found myself asking.

'Who, Colin?' she said, as if he had never been mentioned. The burst had perhaps been private. 'Four or five years, I suppose.'

That would put him in the category of an old friend? I felt relieved. Or of an old lover?

'Goodnight,' she said. 'And thanks.'

I asked her for her name. Marie O'Hara, she said, and gave me a Welbeck number. And then she disappeared into all those halls. Faced with a certainty, for the house was very certain, her mystery deepened.

II

WHEN I saw her next—after a week's
restraint, for I had reason to avoid the
kind of entanglement, love or infatuation,
that her personality promised—I asked her directly
whether or not she was in love with this Colin.

After a pause for raised eyebrows, at first un-
assumed, then continued in artifice as she took time to
consider her answer, she said: 'A long time ago I
stopped myself falling in love with him. And so never
did.'

Such a statement is suspect on anyone's lips.
Many a romantic impulse might lie beneath it. But
then—was I not doing the same thing towards her,
by not telephoning, by 'stopping myself falling in
love'?

I had reached a time in life when I thought I knew
which were the women dangerous to my private and
personal equilibrium. I did not want to fall in love. I
was in love with a dream of the work I didn't do.

So there we were the two of us at the same thing—
she stopping herself loving Colin, I stopping myself
loving her. A timorous triangle indeed; but perhaps in
tune with these tamer times? Throw the wild things
overboard—violence, drunkenness, oppression—and
you throw overboard the spirits to surmount them, the

spirits gay and chivalric. These are considered days: we measure before we act. We kill with a thousand-yard shot rather than twist a man on the end of a sword, we buy boned and frozen lamb rather than chops warm from the slaughter house.

And love is getting like that. Considered economics douse the lion with mouse-thoughts. One reason for keeping myself away from thoughts of marriage was that I felt myself unable to support a wife in the manner to which I am accustomed. And, though I achieved a fair income from playing the piano in various ways, at recording sessions, as an accompanist, and as an occasional orchestral arranger, as well as tinkering at the Marlven, I still thought of myself as a potential composer, and a fairly serious one at that: the rest was a bridge to this end. But so far, for all my thirty years, nothing had been either published or even performed. So although it looked as if I had 'time and money', I had not overmuch of the second and very little indeed of the first. The freedom of a free-lance is more circumscribed than is imagined: one does two jobs, those of both master and slave. Too much time is spent asking oneself permission to take a day off, and regretfully refusing.

And all this is more or less what Marie and I talked of that evening in her flat.

For I got there. And much sooner than I had ever expected.

We met at the New Marlven. It was again not one

of my playing nights: I must have suggested the same place out of habit or because of credit.

So there we sat among the well-known damasky walls and renewed our acquaintanceship. A gold-framed convex mirror hung on the opposite wall and in this I watched our two figures made miniature and bright, most intimate, lensed together in a camera eye.

O second meetings! After the joyful intoxication of the first—this covert sizing up, this fearful knowledge that no more is it chance, but now an agreement to spend time together. And how should this time be spent? Searching for common ground—a serious effort. Seeing clearly for the first time. Noticing imperfections in the mirage: and it is upon the reception of these imperfections that the matter turns.

One has been told that true love 'loves for the lover's faults'. What more often seems to happen is that love chooses to ignore faults and consciously to exaggerate virtue. The ballooning of illusion smooths the way long before the truest love, child of habit and time, may properly flower.

Pretending objectivity but letting the illusion grow, fascinated but consciously respectful, I sat and consumed Miss Marie O'Hara (Turkish?). Nowadays, it is customary to think in measurements. 'Do you know my wife—35–34–40?' This O'Hara was a small woman, not much over five foot three: and her overall figures were, as I later learned, 34–20–34. Charming little locomotive! Such figures remind me of the days when as boys we had our brains filled with the wheel-setting of railway-engines—a 4-4-2 or a 2-6-4—not forgetting, as with Marie, the 'tender behind'. Do I sound coarse? That's because I am. There are other assessments to be made alongside a beautiful respect for the soul.

Her dark blue eyes stared as straight and composed as ever: a few freckles, umber on paler brown, gave the blue a certain indistinction—as if her eyes swam in something not so solid as flesh. She still looked like a mouse: most people have the breath of an animal like-ness—all those hippo-men, fish-boys, fowl-faced women, and girls like little frogs—and Marie looked like a mouse with a sense of humour. Her upper lip shivered as with whiskers, but it was only fun.

She was dressed soberly, smartly in grey—but tonight her skin did not look so brown. How is it that a brown dress brings out brown, and also a white dress brings out brown?

She had a dirty neck—the kind a woman gets from a dyed black dress, widow's grime. Had she rushed, after a quick change, from the office? Did she work hard, or was this a mark of the slut? Diligent? Dilatory?

She refused a second drink before absolutely finish-ing her first; but a third she accepted halfway through her second: a fourth she refused absolutely. I tried to work this out, but did not seem to learn much.

Then Belle came over and paused a moment by our

table, giving me a good-evening and Marie a quick all-over glance. She had remembered the missing pepper-pot and fork, and was taking no risks. 'You don't need these, do you?' she asked, taking up the silver on the table, polite but not waiting for an answer.

As she went away, I said to Marie, to cover any suspicion: 'Colin's ding-dong the other night has been heard here before. About a billion times. We've been through the lot. Jingle Bells is her tune. Belle's Hells her memoirs. We call her Old Tom.'

'To her face?'

'That would be tricky. She's nice but touchy. Never before she's had a drink, and certainly never when she's full up. Catch her when she's filling.'

'Why did she take those things away?'

Oh, sharp.

'Colin?' she said.

I nodded and pulled a face to hide my embarrass-ment:

'I happened to see him do it.'

She pursed her lips and looked almost ugly for a moment.

'And you told?'

'Oh no. They must have been missed, though.'

'Oh that idiot! Always trouble.'

'Does he often—?'

She looked sly herself, sideways and ashamed: 'It's half a kind of kleptomania: and more than half with Uncle's in mind.' And brightly: 'But tell me more about Belle. And the others—in this rather extra-ordinary place?'

I was only too pleased to oblige, fearing at the mention of Colin a repetition of her previous outburst.

'No, you tell me,' I said. 'Tell me about him, for instance!' And I pointed to slick young Andrew up at the bar.

'He's got a nice girl after him,' she said, 'whom he courts when he's broke. Otherwise he's off to the palais, where he stands at the male end licking his lips. One paternity order. He's careful now.'

'He breeds budgies,' I said, 'and practically nothing else.'

She pointed over to Otto and Myra Adrian: 'And they,' she said, 'have a nice little dry-cleaning business. The lady dreams of a launderette, you know.'

That 'you know'. *Wissen Sie, vous savez*—all the time one felt a breath, nicely tweeded, of The Continent.

'And you the daughter of your old Dad! They're in Delight.'

'Of *course*.'

A tall man with a shaved head, huge purple shadows beneath his eyes, a leather strap on his wrist and an extraordinary deep voice, as if there were an artificial speak-machine inside him, thumped up to the bar. 'White-slaver, tobacco-runner,' she said, 'some people would say. But not me. He's in powder-puffs.'

'Nearly. As a matter of fact, it's Raoul the *coiffeur*.'

She shut her eyes and asked me to play.

To appear to please her—she had said she liked french-window-and-summer-lawn Chopin or a sexy bit of Bach—I began a nocturne. After a while the room stopped talking; there was a restless silence, and when I had finished, even applause. I tried another; but I could feel it really made them uneasy. The tinkle of glass and the squirt of soda were plainly absent, and Belle came over and said: 'For Christ's sake stop it, you'll put me out of business.'

I wandered into a couple of popular tunes, and then shut the lid.

'Very nice,' Marie said, 'you play very well. Now let's go.'

'Oh dear—'

'No—but haven't we had enough of here? It's a bit over-whelming. Where *do* they all come from?'

'Where did you come from? Because they live near.'

I nearly said because they live in stifling little box-flats, because they're childless, because they've no taste for pubs and little of any other kind—but stopped, for after all one or other of these things might have applied to her.

'I came out of curiosity,' she said. 'You can't live somewhere and see these frosted glass doors and see New Marlven written up and not know. Not when it's on your doorstep.'

'Shall we eat something?' I said.

We had got our coats. It was early.

'I'd love to.'

But when I started asking her what restaurant, she interrupted:

'Why not come up to me—talking of doorsteps? If you can bear something scrambled up quick. Saves money, you know.'

Oho!

But on second thoughts, not so very oho. For she had asked *me* up. I had not persuaded her to ask me up. She had not 'given in', foreshadowing a climate of greater concessions. She had conceded nothing, particularly with that mention of money, but straight good fellowship.

There was a time, a golden age, when such an invitation could be taken to mean one thing only. Now it only raises hope, doubt and a crippling sense of honour—burning up our nerves in the names of progress and civilisation. The first war started and the second confirmed these habits of emancipatory restraint. Nowadays, a man must be expected to pass the night alone beneath the same roof, and even, since roofs are limited, in the same room, with a nice friendly girl—and never make the move that was once thought natural. If he does, he may expect to be called a satyr or a beast; and not only called one, *thought* one. The new biology also expects, under certain jolly beach conditions, a man to bathe naked with his comradely lady—and raise not even an eyebrow.

Yet that is not all. If it were only as simple as that,

with a plain ruling! But there is no rule. The position is terribly fluid. He might equally be expected to make his move. And if he does not—and not all women make their desires clear at once—there is the fury of scorn to be borne. Or one is quickly labelled homo-sexual. Though this latter, in the long run, is a hopeful sign, for conversion may then occupy her mind to the exclusion of all else.

So what racks the nerves is the indecision, the fluidity, the suspense. When I was a very young man, I was told that if a woman tickled with her finger the palm of one's hand—or if you were in Vienna and she blew out the match held to her cigarette or cigar—something was indicated. I have waited for years for one or other of these signs to be given me. But in vain: and I can only relegate such precise gestures, like much else, to a golden age disappeared for ever, when there were rules and misconduct, absolute virtue and proper impropriety.

Then if I so disliked the predicament, why did I not insist on a restaurant? Because—need one really ask? —one will suffer any purgatory to reach heaven.

On the way up in the lift, already un-nerved, I find myself talking fast about everything, anything. I even ask her what rent she pays. I cannot judge the figure she gives me in reply—it is just a figure, neither high nor low. Besides, I have not seen the flat yet. She lives on the sixth, the top floor. Outside her flat door stands a single empty milk bottle. I find this tenderly human, terribly intimate.

I receive a glass of South African sherry, and, while with busy steps she goes to rattle things in a little kitchen, am allowed the run of the flat. It is good to be alone.

Walking from object to object, assuming an air of interest but not curiosity, I am surprised to feel that over these diverse objects of her life hangs a little air of death: it is like a museum, or a room which the owner has suddenly left for ever. Even though there are current magazines, scraps of sewing—only her presence will bring these things to life. Meanwhile. I pry about, shaking, sherry-in-hand.

Over to the windows for release. French windows on the sixth floor? The curtains are drawn back and, peering through the room's reflection, I see the reason —a stretch of flat roof walled by gables and high Dutch chimney stacks. Beyond—the moon and starshine of an intensely clear and brilliant night of frost. Frost glitters on the roof, on all the roofs scattered beyond like the humble huddle of a hill-town seen from the castle's eminence. Walls higher than real garden walls, walls curving and gabling to hold the huge chimneys: it is a strange place, Paris comes to mind, and on a clothes-line hung across I spot two slack dead pairs of men's socks. Men's? Why not hers? Women wear socks with trousers? But jealousy and possession have already taken root. These socks mar the glittering night, they hang large as gibbeted hares against the neon-flushed rose and indigo sky: they are big, far too big for her small sparrow feet. Turning back to the room, I find it has come alive—this is a place where things happen, where people lead lives I do not know about.

Then she comes in, jacketless, in a sweater that pumps out two agonizing taut breasts—and I look away hurt. I cannot meet the eyes of these breasts. Where have they been before? Whose hands do they know? Eyes! One talks to the real eyes and casually drops one's own—and there's the other two, the pop-eyes, exactly beneath, staring right out at you.

'So here you see how the poor live!'

My own eyes search for something with which to combat this sudden brightness. There are a few pleasing but unexceptional Victorian chairs, a new flowered wallpaper, bookcases, books in them, a little Wedgwood and even, in a dark corner, a Van Gogh. Normal. Unpretentious. And as the pause lengthens I turn my eye in anguish upwards, where they come to rest on the pendant white nipple of a disused electric lighting fixture, an alarming triplet to add to the others. It is like a nightmare flight, with a police-man popping up at the end of every street.

'What a pretty Wedgwood vase,' I manage from memory.

An omelette is put before me. The outside is firm as eggy doeskin, but it wobbles at the fork-touch, and a drop of buttery orange yolk oozes out. Good for my hostess! I comment on this. No messy deprecations—she thanks me for my praise. Easier now. I try a nearly nonchalant look at her chest. But how long will an omelette take to eat? Staring at us from the other side of the room, empty, wickedly innocent, lies a body-length settee.

What will come after? Cheese? Fruit? Pudding? I long for some protracted dish—we could crack nuts, for instance, for hours. Meanwhile, we discuss the roof garden and how the sun hits it, our mutual wish for a strengthened Liberal party, and a new play neither of us has seen but of which we know enough to debate away ten precious minutes. She seems to be at ease; her dark blue eyes smile and twinkle at me with what seems to be pleasure—but she passes the salt twice. Has she no faith in this omelette?

It is possible that she is as troubled as I am. We are both in the same boat. Having sung out her invitation on the spur of a cordial moment, she now has to face an older music played by four uncompromising walls.

'We live in a cock-eyed world, a cart-before-the horse life,' I hear myself saying. 'Technology outpaces technique, amorality leads to immorality . . . the future occurs before the present.'

And I am dining with an attractive woman? I am supposing myself half-in-love?

Suddenly she goes out and comes back with two immense flans. She remarks: 'Do you skate?'

I do not skate. Must I skate to win her? I feel the uncomfortable sensation of a man expected to gird his loins, and catch a quick glimpse of myself on my bottom in a rink full of bright-coloured serenely sailing young people, while jazz echoes round and round from a loudspeaker.

Later, as finally we move from the table towards the electric fireplace, I grow wild: 'My Monster film,' I say, working myself up, 'will feature a thousand-foot high blonde in a giant bathing costume striding up from the Gulf of Mexico into Galveston, Tex., crushing Cadillacs beneath her house-high heels. She is Atlanta, risen with a golden rinse from the Deep. The big moment comes when you see her staggering across the entire breadth of the United States with the limp body of a crewcut USAAF lieutenant clutched to her four-hundred-foot bust. Death agony is from a fissile missile disguised by the lieutenant's girl, a champion of clean-cut American womanhood always in and out of the lab, as a rocket-size lipstick.'

Have I gone too far—I mean, with that about the bust? Not a bit of it. She sniggers—and goes to draw the curtains. I have a last vision of those two dark dead socks silhouetted against the Milky Way. I would prefer a whole line of socks to the dreadfully drawn curtains that now so formally enclose us. Wildly, I go on about my Thing.

How is it, then, that within half-an-hour we are sitting on the settee in each other's arms?

37

At what point can this have happened?

I am quite sure that nothing could have been *said*. We must have gone straight from some impersonal talk into an embrace—our chemical bodies drawn together by eye-flickers, lip-quivers, odours and other attractions as nearly impalpable to our conscious senses as the bee's visionary violet.

With absolute composure she removes her earrings and places these neatly on a side-table. It is the calm automatic gesture of a task done every day, or night. Instant depression drops hollow inside me: but it passes quickly. Somehow, perhaps by an unspoken surrender implicit in her very composure, as if this were ordained between us, she has made her action personal to ourselves; or have I?

Soon, but long after the light raspberry taste of lipstick has been swallowed and forgotten—soon even the secret of the socks has lost its power. Rather, it is I who have taken charge of this room: whatever secrets it holds are old, discarded things, socks with holes in them.

How much, on such an occasion, a woman gives! The extent of the armour that is shed in one moment is truly considerable—all the coolnesses, the formalities, the composures, all the innumerable small restraints she wears as a daily defence in her role of the chased one! The prim way she sits, as if she is not sitting. The automatic pull to the skirt. The aversion of the eyes. Every day she must go through such disavowals of a body which, one must remember, nobody but she has painted and dressed to suggest so many saliencies. Two creatures in one, as if a disapproving old white-nosed ewe lived inside the body of another sheep black as your hat. Yet the ewe is silenced at one stroke!

So Marie was in my arms. Breathing the intimate smells of her skin and hair, I felt I embraced a treasure of unbelievable, tender value. I would protect it, warm it, fondle it, eat it. It was a clean feeling, very nearly spiritual.

The lights are still on—yet we exist in the shade of our own closeness. Difficulties of conversation have been reduced to mumblings and cooings. Only occasionally the mouthing of a word—Darling, or Oh.

But now a further shadow rises. Where do we go from here? Such a situation is not static.

I have said, How much does a woman give! And now must be added: How much does she retain! Dark intuitions tell me that one false move may now altogether destroy an advance with which I should be thankfully content. Words, hitherto spurned, must be brought to the rescue. I must calm her with words, reassure her, while time inures us to the unaccustomed enlacement of our nervous bodies.

And it is then that, searching for something to say, human indiscretion overcomes these inhuman strategies, the dark deep octopus of the id comes slobbering up all over me and I ask her—of all things—whether she is in love with Colin.

One has read often enough the words: 'She stiffened in his arms.' That is exactly what happened. She did not move away, she simply grew stiff in my arms.

'The mucous membrane of the stomach', write Wolf and Wolff of their gastroscopic observations, 'changed in colour with the emotional state of its owner, now flushing a fiery red, now blenching to a pallid grey.' Too much attention to the soul makes us forget these violent automatisms of our body, ceaseless battles to and fro of agents whose dispatches never reach the brain. After these millennia of human wisdom, of cathedrals and philosophies, how much of man remains animal? Nine-tenths? 'She stiffened in my arms!' As well say: 'She turned grey, or red, all over inside.'

And how, one may be driven to enquire, can a man write thus about the intimacies of his love? The answer is a simple one. Precisely because I *am* in love. In *love*. And I think and wonder about it, about what is really happening rather than what I would wish to happen. I will not say that this is right. It is simply one of the symptoms of desperation.

Her answer came only after a long pause:

'Rather—take it that a long time ago I stopped myself falling in love with him.'

And then another pause before: 'And so never did.'

This second pause, with its breath for thought,

histrionic or diplomatic thought, instantly places a doubt on the message that follows.

The socks retake possession of the room.

And can it be embarrassment, or simply politeness, that makes her now say: 'And *you*? Have you been in love? *Are* you in love? Why—for all I know you might be married! You're a man I met in a club.'

I make my hand do the work of words. Like a faithful little brush, it sweeps her question away. But the tongue is at it again: 'Whose socks,' I ask, 'are those?'

'What?'

'Hanging on the line outside?'

We both stare at the curtains, as if we could see through them. 'Actually,' she says—and what worlds of compromise and dubiety lie in that much used word—'Colin's.'

'Oh.'

'Well—he lives in digs. I help him out now and then.'

I try: 'That's very sweet of you,' and half mean it. 'No lady of his own?' I add.

'There's Eileen.' And with a laugh: 'But I can scarcely see Eileen at the washbowl. Except on a stand.'

'A washhandstand?'

'An exhibition stand. Eileen demonstrates. Anything. Including her own person. One week she's showing off a new cake-mixer, the next she's dressed as a space-girl firing killer-ray bombs at the School-boys' Exhibition. At present she's the Ozal girl at Cruft's.'

'Yes? And she's Colin's "regular"?'

'In so far as that is conceivable.'

She still seems amused—at least she smiles at the idea of Eileen. Are there wives who similarly smile at the idea of a husband's particularly trite mistress?

'As a matter of fact, I'm going to Cruft's tomorrow to see her,' she adds. 'Why not come? You can look at the dogs too.'

London seems full of the most alarming possibilities —skating, dogs. 'Well—yes', I say, 'I'm free in the afternoon.'

'Good.'

And then: 'I *must* get those socks in—I'd quite forgotten.'

It seems very natural for her now to rise and go over to the window. We have been sitting quite relaxed again, talking of Colin's affairs, a comradely feeling has overcome us.

Only the sudden buzzing of the telephone, quietly urgent, like a small creature tiptoeing forward two feet at a time, shows me the absurdity of all this. From the open curtains she now crosses into the bedroom, picks up the receiver and shuts the door, leaving me in the salutary cold.

Buh-buh-buh-buh-buh goes her muttered voice from behind the closed bedroom door. This door was previously ajar, revealing the awful presence of the bed—but after her opening hello she has closed it, casually, with a foot. Kicked it to. Shut me out.

Buh-buh-buh-buh. Up and down it drones, no word clear. I can only sit and look at the socks. Unconsciously I find myself smoothing my jacket, stiffening my tie. Why? Is it all over? Have I failed? Or have I escaped? It is difficult to know. Besides, might it not start up again?

It is all over. There is a long, uneasy interval between the ringing down of the telephone and Marie's return to the room. When she comes in, it is with a blanket clasped in her arms.

'Look—I'm sorry, but I've got to put someone up. You'll have to go. Do you think me frightfully rude?'

Who is this formal creature fussing about the divan with a blanket, so that I have to get swiftly to my feet, make myself scarce?

'Not at all,' I say. 'But can't I help you?'

She does not even hear: 'It's always the same. A damn confounded nuisance.'

At last she seems to remember me: 'Anyway, if you still want to come, we'll see each other tomorrow at the dogs. I suppose *he*'—and her finger points to the blanket, six foot of phantom furled on the divan—'will be there too.'

'Colin?'

'Don't speak to me of Colin. Just don't mention his name.'

'Colin,' I say, 'Colin Colin Colin.'

But she looks so miserable that I must ask more gently:

'What's happened then?'

'Oh, moonlight flit I suppose. Or he's been chucked out. Oh darling, I'm sorry.'

She looks at me tenderly again, with a loving lost longing look—as if I were something pleasant disappearing round the bend of a railway line.

I bend down to kiss her. She smells the same. But she kisses me without thinking, she is miles away. I might be her husband.

It is time to be off.

III

ON the way to Cruft's the next afternoon, I I am still trying to make sense of the night before.

The morning's session, a recording with Sam Paris, has left me more than ever confused. Chorus-verse-vocal-eightbars-solo-and-last-chorus and I have five minutes break to think that at least they don't sleep together, if she made up the divan.

And then the clarinet has to come close up to the mike, and this is all adjusted, and they try it against a solo tom-tom—and I have sixteen bars rest in which to think: But was the blanket a cover for her reputation rather than for his body—which really went to bed beside her? It was feasible, even forgivable. She didn't *know* me, after all.

Then off we go again, the Boys in their hexagonal specs and leisure jackets, some even in bedroom slippers still. O so beautiful the Boys in the morning after playing in restaurants and clubs all night! O how readily the violins and guitar—a split second after the last romantic twangs of *Lilac Memory* have faded to silence—break for coffee and a crap game! Think of this when you are moved to tears by your next long, long player.

But now we're off again with *A Little White Doll*

called Dolly, Hebrew harmonies and Mississippi plonking in a bright American Nursery atmosphere, and as I batter away I remember for the fortieth time what really worries me most of all—why did I go into that deep and perfect sleep the moment my head hit its rightful pillow? Deep, hoggish sleep; not even a dream. Surely I should have stayed awake reliving the agonies of frustration, recounting the moments of bliss? A sense of embarrassed shame overcomes me. I muff a cue, and *A Little White Doll called Dolly* has to be done all over again.

We had agreed to meet inside the Exhibition Building, at Bingate's Pest Bungalow. This was a green-painted, roughcast tudor cottage through whose windows could be seen stacks of pest-killer cartons, crates of flea powder. She was there, by the lych-gate, waiting for me.

But how changed she was, roughened by tweeds, a kind of deer-stalker on her brown hair! Why do they, whose first insistence is on a personal inner *me*, always mess themselves about so? To be everyone at once? She looked quite a different woman and—I must confess the immediate feeling—not too good at all. But possibly these clothes had a simpler message for me: Back to start. Begin all over again.

However—swallowing this small disloyalty, I walk forward and we greet each other.

'Hello.'

'Why, hello!'

A lover's greeting.

'Eileen's by the Afghans,' she says.

'Oh? Is she?'

But our eyes are glancing in and out of each other, shy, friendly, searching, both intimate and reticent, and a great liking like big bright laughter eases me all over inside. I feel suddenly twice my size, brim with pleasure, and throw caution to winds: 'Let Eileen stay with the Afghans! Let's go somewhere and talk.'

And all by itself: 'Darling.'

Deerstalker, tweeds, lych-gate all dissolve and her smile is soft and pleased and understanding. We are together again.

Hand in hand we thread our way through the chattering barking crowd to a kind of exposed inlet, brightly sprayed with pink and gold paint, where people are sitting and calmly drinking alcohol at after three o'clock of an Anglo-Saxon afternoon: men of different kinds drinking beer or whisky; ladies, foxed by the hour, sipping gins-and-oranges.

What we now say to each other no one will ever know, the least ourselves. These are not words, but sounds made to accompany the movements of our faces. In defiance of everything, of uniforms, people, and the din of a thousand dogs, I take her hand in mine, and it stays there, soft in its suède glove, like a warm little ferret.

But I do remember that I avoided mentioning the previous evening. And how dishonest this slight diplomacy seemed! Cannot one ever be absolutely straightforward? But in a way it proved that the situation was too valuable to risk. How many white, ivory, off-white, dove-grey lies we would tell each other—each one a stone in the monument of our building devotion! The hell with Truth; Long live Delusion!

'Will Mr. or Mrs. Parkhurst of Dollis Hill please come immediately to the Elkhounds where their little boy Jimmy's been found lost?'

The amplifier repeats this a second time with an impatient emphasis on *Park*hurst. All of us in the bar, drinking guilty alcohol in the middle of the afternoon, look questioningly at each other. Who's a Parkhurst? You? You? *You*! It reminds us of Eileen, and we rise to leave. This is a mistake. We are instantly marked down as the defecting Parkhursts.

The enormous belly of the hall, tiered with upper floors, misted with blue smoke and the glass-domed echo of thousands talking and barking, gives the impression of a vast Assembly Room in which a hundred cock or dog fights are being held at once. In all directions separate circles of macintoshed and tweeded backs hide each particular event. Occasionally the amplifier, godlike master of ceremonies, intones a general message to hearten us: and then one imagines that everyone should change places, as in musical chairs. A smell of biscuit, sawdust and doggy fur hangs thick in the air.

We get mixed up in one of the circles. An ordinary-looking man extraordinarily briskly walks to and fro holding out at arms-length a lead with a morose-looking hound on the end of it. He walks hard across the open space towards the wall of spectators. He won't, he can't, he'll *never* stop himself—he's going straight through! But at the last moment he brakes, turns, and swings off again. That man's eyes are fixed on a middle distance quite his own. He is a fanatic, a visionary. The dog, a Red Setter, looks half-mad too —it is one of those dogs whose long rear portion walks to one side, hurrying to catch up with the poor crazed fore-quarters. A few judges, rosetted, equipped with comfortable stick-seats, mumble to each other and write in their books with nearly naval nonchalance, ignoring the man who is once again off at a brisk trot towards his visionary moorland of macintoshes. As Marie now whispers to me: 'Who's going to have hard-pad after this?'

We press on past a row of wired hatches containing white and brown dogs with sad topheavy heads, Basset Hounds, *wasserköpfe* of the dog world: past a row of Spaniels, red-eyed and wigged as hanging judges: past a frisk of Pomeranians: past Bedlingtons like long-legged lizards worked in wool, past a dragon display of Pekingese Terriers. Past Fox-terriers, past lost youth.

'You mustn't be too surprised by Eileen,' Marie says, 'she's an odd girl, but sweet at bottom. And she's awfully good to Colin.'

But here she is. By the Afghans. And a sight for which I am certainly not prepared.

To begin with, Eileen is dressed in an emerald uniform as some superior kind of air-hostess. And from the fine brass instrument she carries, one gathers that she is the one who blows the hunting horn at the back of the aeroplane. But this is no more, on closer acquaintance, than the Ozal Gun. Under her jaunty forage-cap Eileen is as heavily painted and luxuriously coiffeured as a professional odalisque: except that no professional, knowing her business is to improve upon rather than occlude Nature, would ever have gone so far.

Eileen is a white-skinned redhead. Over her white skin she has painted another and a whiter skin, and against the brilliantined red of her hair she has drawn deep black lashes and eyebrows, a few black spots, and lips of permanganate purple. Her hair, luxuriant and crisply waved, spreads wide over her shoulders and down her back, a real Irish mat, more 'marcelled' than 'permed'. Gitana curls, thin as copper wire, are glued to her cheeks and temples. She is a handsome girl, but the final effect is of an articulated and exquisite wax head from a hairdresser's window. Golden beer-barrels hang from her ears, she has a silver tooth, and a number of rings sparkle on her fingers. Stronger than any disinfectant she might carry in her little brass gun, there hangs about her a heavy smell of white night-flowers.

'Hi,' says Eileen. 'Welcome to purgatory.'

A promising beginning. Her eyes flutter open and shut, which gives them a kind of dollish glitter. But after the first effusion of greeting it becomes noticeable that Eileen prefers the monosyllable. 'Uh' is one, and 'Huh' another. She is affable, but on show—it is like addressing a queen. Each 'uh' is conferred as a blessing: each 'huh' the contempt royal.

After a while, Marie has to go to the Powder Room and I am left alone with my new emerald friend. Searching for some little piece of general knowledge, I point to one of the long silken-haired Afghans propped up in his baggy trousers against the wire behind us: 'You wouldn't think these elegant creatures were lion-hunters, would you?'

'Uh?'

'That's what they were bred for.'

'Huh.'

'Two of them can bring a lion down. They go for the hind legs.'

'I dunno. I don't like dogs much.'

The Afghan surveys us with disdain: but he is no match for Eileen, who has not even bothered to look his way.

'Bad luck then, being mixed up with them,' I try.

'Oh, I couldn't care less.'

'Now what, Eileen—I'm sorry, I don't know your other name—do you *really* like?'

'I don't mind.'

But she has been asked about herself. It is irresistible. Her purple lips open like indelible pencil-suckings to add:

'I don't like dogs. Smelly things. Leaving their hairs all over everyone. I like boys.'

It seems to be all she has to say. But no—the heavy silence that underlines this pregnant ukase is simply a pause for breath as the two indelible lips roll back for a flooded inventory straight from the heart:

'—and cars, and jive, and going places and lots of things, and cars, and, well, boys and fun, and swimming, I know what I like and I'm not afraid to say so, not *me*!'

She has pulled herself up, and blazes out a final indignation:

'And I don't care *who* knows it!'

My fatal enquiry seems to have cast me for the role of watch committee. I stand there the symbol of years of parental stricture. And make haste to stutter:

'Good for you then!'

'Huh,' she says, not fooled.

Luckily I catch sight of Marie on her way back from the Powder Room. And as I wave, hear the voice at my side unaccountably add: 'One thing I will say . . . I-like-the-way-a-hound-holds-his-tail.'

Surprising reconciliation!

But it is not Eileen, only a tiny crop-haired lady in tweeds and a pork-pie hat. Eileen has stalked off, head high, squirting her gun to right and to left with magnificent indifference.

'Colin's got his hands full there,' I mutter to Marie coming up. 'Wherever did he find her?'

'In a garage.'

'A—?'

'It's a long story,' she giggles.

'I'm all ears.'

Then she looks serious.

'It's not so funny really. Anyway you'd never believe it. It's Colin all over.'

She bites her lip, looks sideways at me—she wants to tell a secret but must make at least the motions of keeping it. 'Do you know what a petrol-sniffer is?' she asks.

'No?' Though vaguely the phrase is familiar.

'It's quite serious really, it's an addiction to the smell of petrol—like any other narcotic. People who work among petrol fumes get the habit. Colin got it. It's just like him to fall for a second-rate kind of drug like that.'

'But you surely wouldn't want him to—'

'Of course not. I'm only saying that it's in character for him to choose some sort of off-beat thing like that.'

'Well—one doesn't choose such things.'

'Two opinions there. He let it choose him, didn't he? Anyway, he's only got it mildly. For which thank the heavens—because it can send you mad, it can kill you. I think he used to hang around the racing pits once—something like that. Anyhow, one day he's up at some coffee-stall and along comes Eileen in her white overalls.'

'Her white what?'

'Eileen was one of those angels in white overalls at the more recherché garages who serve out the gas and so on. I think they called her Annie Lorry in those days. In fact, Eileen smells of petrol: Colin smells Eileen: Love is born.'

'It's not true.'

'Honestly, he gets hooked with Eileen because he likes to sniff her. Of course, she's a good-looker, too.'

'But now that she's left the garage?'

'I suppose she's become a habit, too.'

'Second-rate?'

'Don't try to catch me.'

And then here was Colin himself, clipped moustache and plastered hair, smiling his way between breeders and fanciers, red-eyed dogs and rheumy newsmen.

'Speak of the Devil,' I said.

But it was the Kaiser, as always with Colin, who came to mind. Puttied subalterns in the Palm Lounge of the Piccadilly. Passchendael and the medals and chicken farms that followed—one could not get away from these as Colin's clipped, battered, charming face came forward.

'Hello hello *hello*,' cries Colin, manfully pumping

my hand. 'Apologies for the other night, a bit the worse for wear.' And turning to Marie, he possesses her with a big look: 'Hello, *darling*'—with a quick and amused little glance at me to see what effect this may have.

I take this with what I imagine to be impeccable equanimity—though who knows what strange pictures the face, quite by itself, draws?—and beam with charm. So! Is there something feminine beneath this leathern hide, that he should wish to manœuvre a 'situation'?

A moment later Eileen strolls up, shooting as she comes, and at Colin's suggestion we move over to one of the beer bars nearby. There he adroitly kills three birds with one stone. Such is his flow of words upon Marie that Eileen is stimulated, my own discomfort grows, and since he is so busy talking it is I who am left to pay for the drinks.

'What a mob, what an *atmosphere*!' he chants. 'It's Market Day, isn't it? Exactly! Doesn't it come back, darling—motoring in from Yattendon, the pubs open, a frosty afternoon, the smell of farmers. Remember old Suckling?'

So they have lived together in the country? A holiday? In *winter*? The shaft goes home, my jealousy is roused. Yattendon! Old Suckling! Such names evoke for me a golden age, a rich and carefree past lived by these two, hero and heroine, at some perfect and mysterious level unattainable forevermore. Vainly

I tell myself that whatever happened must have been marred by reality. But the dream masters my sanguinity—Yattendon! Old Suckling!—I am lost in one of man's liveliest melancholies, golden agery, hope turned backwards. When a child listens to the downstairs gaiety of grown-ups, he wants not just to grow up but to grow up there and then. No waiting. It is because he can never do this, but must wait until the years have spoiled illusion, that he will never ever truly experience a golden moment. Nothing will ever be as good as what he missed. Yattendon and Old Suckling bred in me a similar sense of loss, there among the dogs, the beer, Colin's memories.

Marie, indeed, tempered the story. She spoke of the awful little attic room, full of bicycles, which he had been given in the farm where, as guests of his aunt, they had stayed. But all I saw was the passage between that attic and her room, the night, the pad of bedroom slippers along the linoleumed corridor.

'I shall get copped if I stay here any longer.'

Eileen was restive.

Colin went on with what he was saying. He had got round to a summer visit by now. 'We couldn't believe our eyes. They were the perfect bride and groom, he so black and his consort well and truly veiled. A sweep and a beekeeper! Coming out of the little old country church—on a summer's day! You never saw *anything* like it. God knows what they were doing there.'

A grunt from Eileen. 'And who wants to and what's so wonderful?'

'But, sweetie, don't you *see* . . .'

'What's the fuss? A sweep and a man for bees.'

'You lack a soul, dear.'

'Bees!' Eileen's top lip curls right up with contempt like a sliver of bacon hitting a hot pan. 'Soot!'

'You remind me,' Marie interrupted, 'wasn't it De Quincey, who tells us about bees and chimneys? How they extract their materials indiscriminately from roses and soot?'

My erudite, peacemaking darling! We all look round surprised at this sudden information. Eileen raises her eyes to the glass roof—it is too much. Colin giggles, tosses back his beer and suggests we move on. No question of another round.

We all follow him—somehow he continues to hold our attention. Of what is Colin's charm composed? Of a smile, of the kind called boyish, easy and radiant. And strong-cut dimples—permanent recesses of good nature, whatever he is feeling. A commanding eye, an alive eye, quick and watchful. Colin is also a good listener, even when he is talking, as most of the time, about himself. Cleverly he welcomes your personality into his, you are received and feel complimented.

'Lady Foley de Witt to the gundogs!' booms the amplifier.

'Poor woman,' we shudder, 'a terrible end.'

Things are getting tittery. A nearby collie points its

long nose to the roof like a booming bittern and begins to howl. Its throat quivers with hairy emotion as the awful noise, part yawn and part pain, bellows up and all around. 'Once bittern,' I begin, but nobody will get it.

Then Eileen stops stockstill by a table exhibiting rubber biscuits and rubber bones. She stands transfixed, her mascaraed eyes wide with wonder. The biscuits lie in rows like little white mattresses, the red rubber bones like big dried giblets. 'Now these,' says Eileen, 'are really clever, aren't they? Aren't they clever?' she says.

It is the first time that Eileen has shown any real interest this afternoon. The biscuits seem to stir her deeply indeed. Her wavy-haired wax head pores over the stiff white biscuits—and at last one can see something of her trouble. Eileen has probably thirty different jobs a year: she works in all circumstances, in the oddest surroundings—one week at Ozal, the next in a mink bikini up in Leeds. Odd? No longer to her. She has seen too much of it. She has found that one way of exorcising madness is to take it seriously. Like a stock exchange man and his risqué anecdote, his Irishman-and-a-Scotsman-and-a-Jew, Eileen needs her fun dressed up to look like fun: she takes life formally, she has a genuine need for biscuits made of rubber.

We go on past the Schnautzers, past dazzling Dalmatians and ratlike Papillons. Every movement of Eileen's body, leading us, is artificially co-ordinated:

her short-stepping high heels bump up her calves, and these brace her bottom, which then swings free to left and right, when the waist takes over and sets the shoulders jangling: it is not only life that Eileen takes seriously—untold hours have been spent before the glass, she is as combed and cropped and articulated as any of the prize hounds we pass.

Colin suddenly falls silent. For a few seconds, this is a relief. But it becomes uncomfortable: and I am panicked into saying what men everywhere say to each other at such difficult moments.

'Busy these days?'

I remembered his camera in pawn, and bit my tongue.

'No,' he said, 'not too much. But I've a number of things in view. The trouble is one needs cash, capital, to manage really effectively. On the other hand, you might think a camera and a studio are enough. I've got these, and I roll along. But one needs cash for contacts.'

Marie, who had lagged a little behind, caught up just then: 'Did you get a room this morning, Colin?'

'A room?' he asked.

'Wasn't it rotten luck, Colin's landlord chucked him out last night. Without warning.'

He smiled at me, quite unruffled: 'I've got one in view, just round the corner.'

'Near the old place?' Her eyes were wide with fright. He had plainly left of his own accord, owing rent.

'No, round the corner from you.'

Marie took my arm as she said: 'Well, you'd better get it fixed up, hadn't you?'

He looked at her quickly, then away:

'Course,' he said.

'Your bag's with the porter.'

Now he looked really puzzled.

'Downstairs?'

'Downstairs,' she said.

'Oh, right. I'll pick it up later.'

It was time to go and we had to leave Eileen to finish her shift. Outside the building, in the daily street of traffic and people, a strangely rational world, Colin pulled me back for a second and whispered: 'I say, you couldn't possibly lend me a quid or two, could you? Just over the weekend?'

'Of course. How much would do?'

'A fiver?'

'I'm afraid I haven't that much on me.'

He smiled and said quickly: 'Oh, well, a couple of quid, a quid even? I'm terribly sorry.'

I fingered two pounds in my pocket, and gave him one.

'All right?' I said.

His look of gratitude was so sincere that I handed him the second note.

'Better make it two.'

'Thanks *awfully*.' And when he had put the notes safely away: 'You're sure you can spare it?'

We caught up with Marie and made for the bus stop. Then, as a taxi approached, his hand went up.

'Got to get going,' he said. 'Have a good time!'

The door slammed, his face appeared for a moment bent forward pale in the window, and he was gone. Marie and I were left to walk alone towards our places in the queue.

'He hasn't got a job just now?' I asked.

'No.'

'Nor a room?'

'A room perhaps—certainly no rent money. He's got a bag heavy with books in lieu of that.'

'And now he's got the odd rent money—or what's left after the taxi.'

'How? Yes—how did he get the taxi money?'

I told her.

'Oh dear,' she said.

'It wasn't much. If he's got any sense he'll pay it back—to get more later.'

'My God, he's well past that kind of subtlety by now. You've seen the last of that, I'm afraid.'

I stood there feeling less angry than a fool. I stang with foolishness. It was the bus queue that did it. Here was Colin in a taxi and I, the economic provider, in a bus queue. Yet if I had refused him the money, I would have felt mean. It was unfair.

A little later, in the bus, she suddenly squeezed my hand. 'That was very sweet of you,' she said.

'What?'

'Helping Colin out.'

'It was nothing,' I lied. 'Forget it.'

'But that's just what one doesn't do,' she said, squeezing again.

I expected her to go back to her office. But apparently she had managed the whole afternoon off. 'I'll make it up to them later,' she said, and asked me upstairs for a cup of tea.

The curtains were half-drawn. The last light of the winter's afternoon lit the room dimly. So cold a light contrasted strangely with the heat—the steam pipes must have been on all day.

Without switching on the light, Marie turned and put herself in my arms. We kissed a long black kiss, and then she led me into the bedroom.

There was a sad feeling about the little pause while, in silence, in the half-dark, we undressed. It struck a note nearly of resignation, of patient submission to an irrevocable task—it was like unpacking to go on a journey. And looking over at her in her underclothes, instantly more frail, and her back bent it seemed humbly over her stockings, I felt vaguely sorry about it all. Stripped of the armour of her dress, she seemed to be giving too much.

But she was taking. She pressed herself warmly against me, no breath of refusal, no erection of modesty. Mine, if any, was the modesty—for a long time I remained impotent. Why was this? Was it a fear of failure? Or was it fear of ease?

For what had happened was perhaps altogether too sudden. The whole fabric of society had fallen in a second, a door fitted with the locks of a hundred taboos was suddenly found to be ajar. To attempt to open such a door when locked was natural, and indeed part of the taboo: but to find it loose on its oiled hinges, opening without effort, confounds the energies. It cannot be believed. And a kind of fear arises—that it is not so, or at least that it is the product of a moment's hallucination, which will pass. And not all the softnesses, breaths, light smells, touches of hair and of the warm silk of skin—not all these fine animal affirmations are enough to stop the destructive working of a conscious mind.

Time.

Time to relax into the proper claims of the flesh. Time to become calm enough to believe. Once, as somewhere outside a light was switched on, a shadowed pattern filtered through the lace curtains on to the pillow and showed me her face. This quiet revelation of her, of all the mystery and emotion of the face itself, of the few open inches where all romance and illusion and whatever it is one loves seem to lie visible—this offering, as the light filtered in, of the oval, lipped and starred dream made us real again, and gave back the impetus to consummate the impossible.

Later, the telephone rang.

Eyes opened a moment, then frowned, closed. We were too deeply sunk in peace. The only movement in the room was the buzz of that muffled insistent bell. It went on and on and on: then, with no warning, ceased.

The silence it left was stronger than before, and confirmed us.

IV

THESE are dancing days!—under a drab February sky heavy with snow which never falls. Not a spark of real light glitters life into the chill, dull, grey-brown London pavement: nor, try as I will, do these new excitements gild in the least the familiarly dreary scene. The February drab lumbers on despite us.

Yet inside I wink with action, like an ill-fitted electric bulb shivering on and off.

On and off—could I, after all, not be in love? Could I, being in love, have written so intimately of our first caresses?

I could. I am guilty only of bad manners. Dedicated as we are to the clouds, these are things which one is hardly supposed to admit even to one's self, let alone write down. However, I have written the word 'caresses'. That should be an improvement. It is absurd to say that love stops the mind working. On the contrary, one starts thinking harder than ever before. One does not charge with one's defences down.

I look around my flat and think of hers. Mine I know, hers I don't—there's the big difference. Hers has become unbearably exciting. The Van Gogh—hanging just *there*! That Dutch-gabled roof-garden! Well, I've known others—but they were not hers. All she has is vested with extraordinary value.

E   65

My own flat is a box in a modern pile. I shall never agree that such boxes are impersonal. If anything, they are too personal. Other people's movements can be heard through the walls. Other people's feet fall on the ceiling. A sense of continuing life is transmitted by the bubblings and hammerings of many pipes. Radios switch on and off like musical mice. You meet people in the corridors. And inside the boxes one-two-three along the passage each resident may be known the more sharply for a background of cream walls common to all. Yet 'personality' is supposed to lie in older houses filled with an arbitrary hotch-potch of antiques —third-best choices of secondhand goods. Seldom the first choice—so where's the personality? But now I find this pet argument confounded by the unpretentious assortment in Marie's flat—how these things mark her down, how precious they become!

Appropriately or ironically, I have to spend the morning scoring the guitar part of a love-song: 'Here in your arms / Lost in your charms / The skies opened up and stars fell all around . . .'

Well, it could not be said to feel quite like that. And yet . . . one may remember how such words, at an uncritical moment in a coloured ballroom with a new sweetheart, do their work well. In fact, with a light affair, one *does* charge with defences down? But no—mine now is different, it is heavy, it is worth thinking about.

The fat red bars of the electric fire throw up a

pleasing regular glow, the furred carpet looks warm as an overcoat, the staved paper and black ink on the desk insulate my morning against the window, through which a refreshing little coldness blows. Outside, February: inside, Man.

Totting up. Three meetings and to bed—what does that make her? One must not judge too harshly. Society is looser about these things today: no use balking at the facts, whatever might be wished.

But how many times before? Impossible to judge. One voice says: Many times, for it was certainly she who provoked it. Another says: But wasn't there some slight clumsiness, the awkward movements of the beginner? A third says: Such clumsiness was just greed. And a fourth voice intones: Come clean! Can you quite rule down your ego, that knight in tarnished armour who says: Possibly, just possibly, it was Me?

Impossible to estimate. But one undeniable ray of light beams through—we do not really know much about each other, we have not spent hours babbling about our inner selves. That is indeed hopeful. For however the spark was lit, it was a true spark, chemical and animal, not born of prying and peeking. Let these come later. Their business is to confirm truth, not make it. And another thing—she was the huntress, I the prey: that is as it always is, whatever the masculine story-books say, and it is healthy to have it in the open for once.

The smell of coffee from the percolator, the dull snow, the grey of the clouds, a black-branched winter tree all twigs. My black tadpoles, my musical notes, swim onto the thinly engraved stave-lines—making lute-like guitar chords to throb against three muted cornets coughing gold like a cash register.

But my other mind sings : When that telephone rang, we two were too together for it! The beast defeated! Colin conquered!

Yet a few bars later, my pen hangs suddenly frozen. I stare at my fingers. Those were the same fingers that in the bus were so lightly squeezed when she said: 'How sweet of you to help Colin out!' Colin? Was it all because I'd helped Colin? Had that simple act clocked up the digit 'goodness' in her mind, corroding from the first that true and natural metal I had imagined we forged so purely?

I find myself pacing up and down my muffled room, dangerous as a beast behind bars.

We meet now almost every day. Almost—that keeps us on tenterhooks. Privacies are still maintained. In one way, we are consummated: in another we have a long way to go—we hardly know each other at all. And so we embark upon the tremendous business of never finding out about each other.

Lunch with Eileen and Colin. Four-cornered and claws covered, everyone out for a different object. My growing ambivalence towards Colin: I despair in his presence, yet thirst for him. He knows so much about her. He is chock full of clues. Also, he is a nice enough fellow, if to be pitied and a bit of a bitch. He talks of a year-ago party—from the few things he says, her image comes to me, I see her dress, smell her powder, see her fall over, laugh as she gets up, am thankful it was not too much drink, and even see various pieces of furniture in the room, drawn, of course, from some independent memory of my own.

I hear that she is impatient in shops and always over-buys, she loves the ugliest animals in the zoo, and she has a reverence for old-fashioned convention and manners which she never follows in practice. All these things I learn from Colin.

Eileen gently prods a leaf of lettuce, decorated with slivers of fresh tomato and hardboiled egg, lying on a round of buttered bread. This indigenous assembly goes by the name of a *salada* on the menu. We find ourselves in this dashing department store restaurant, because Eileen is dressed as a milkmaid to help sell a new line of children's country books somewhere downstairs. She tells us how she nearly lost the job because the books were nearly late because the dugs on the cows' udders had to be painted out throughout the edition. A *salada* upstairs, no teats beneath: we sit most civilised here.

The painting and curling of Eileen's face and hair are as fastidious, as coldly perfect as a too well-swept parlour. But it takes all sorts to make a person; outside the door of the courtesan Cora Pearl's country villa lay a mat saying: Wipe Your Feet. Beneath her well-hoovered hair, and her uh-huh façade, Eileen turns out to have not a cold but a pleasant, simple, unassuming mind. She has the dead seriousness of a child, and a child's respect for formality. Her approach to Colin is over-simple, intense and earnest. And Colin can wrap up a few ironical words and confound her completely. He does not do this gratuitously, and on the whole he is very patient; but she does ask for it.

'How d'you like the perm, Colin? You haven't said how you like it. Do you?'

'Yes, Eileen.'

'Well is that all you have to say?'

'No, Eileen.'

'Well then?'

'I think it's a really lovely perm. And the reddy-gold rinse—it's really *rinsey*, isn't it?'

'Rinsey, yes . . .'—and Eileen furrows her brow in thought as this appealing conception forces itself upon her—'yes, I suppose it *is*!'

In general, Colin happens to give as many sidelights on Eileen as he does on my Marie. I nod, smile . . . but while everything seems possible with Eileen—that she has a fine old Irish temper when roused, that she was photographed in the altogether for a heavy-engineering calendar yet refuses to go on the Giant Racer because it blows her skirts about, and so on—

while Eileen's open face made anything credible, Marie's recession belied anything said about her. I could conjure up images of her past, yet never quite believe in them.

She was so poised—as if an insulating current of cool air ran round her all the time. Those dark deep blue eyes could look straight into yours and still retain themselves, seeing something far beyond the obvious. Could this perfect engine over-buy? Impossible. Skate? Incredible. And . . . had she slept in my arms? Absolutely not. She was as intact as ever. Yet there had taken place what is called 'intimacy'!

'May I have the salt, please?'

'Certainly, Marie—here—'

The simple silverish salt-cellar has become an object of ridiculous significance. She pours a little pyramid on the edge of her plate. That she should take salt! And she pours it—like any one else! I am becoming absurd. . . .

As we leave, and pass among the vacant eyes of shoppers lingering about the goods on show, she puts her hand round my arm. Instant intimacy, plugged in like an electric current.

'Darling—how many times before?'

'Inquisitive?'

'Well, there have been others—'

'One or two.'

'But how many?'

71

'What does it matter?'

'It matters to me.'

'A figure?'

'I don't know why but it does.'

'What is it you're after, with your figures?'

We are lying in bed and getting to know about each other. The room is very warm, with steam-heat and a fire, but she has drawn the sheet up over her nakedness. Is this modesty, or a concession to the idea of winter? The sheet fits her like a classic robe, or a shroud; revealing nothing, suggesting all. After a while she raps out a number.

'Oh well, actually three, you know.'

But do I know? Has she not had too much time to think? That 'three' raps out with too much certainty —like a number you are asked for in a game. And, experience tells me, take the number you first thought of and add one or two. One or two are usually forgotten and forgiven, largely in self-defence, as with age-numbers; but partly also because one or two were not truly considered to be lovers—something was not surrendered. Or, that night she was not herself in some way, she was somebody else, it was an error.

Nevertheless I try to believe her, for it is my only evidence. 'Three?' with falling heart. If she had said fifty, I could not have felt worse.

'Three,' she repeated. Her eyes glanced quickly sideways. So it was nevertheless a confession of shame? Good!

But then brightly: 'That's pretty good, considering, isn't it?'

Not so good.

'Considering what?'

'O-oh . . . I'm twenty-eight. And all that. Some of the stories I hear . . . well . . .'

I cannot help being shocked. And hurt, and above all saddened. What is this sad sense of sacrifice that accompanies the idea of a woman giving love? Should it not be glorious?

But I am pulled up short.

'And you?'

'Me? What?'

'How many women, my good man?'

'Oh—I don't know. Not so many.'

'Innumerable?'

'With a man it's different. One forgets.'

'That's pretty ungallant, isn't it? But it's the number that makes you forget—you're all a lot of dirty swine.'

'We're made differently.'

'I'm told there are professional ladies who have three or four different men most nights of the year, year after year—'

'Business is business.'

'—and quite like it!'

'Marie! But by different I mean that *biologically* we're different. Our business is to be promiscuous, whatever society says.'

73

'Society says remain faithful and preserve the family unit.'

'So we're hard put to it, aren't we? We're expected to have two pairs of hands. It encourages the subfusc. There are two kinds of men discussed by society. One is condemned as a lecher, a cad, a promiscuous swine. The other is jovially praised as a "gay old dog". Yet both do exactly the same.'

'Moral—put a cheerful face on it.'

'And which of these am I?'

'You?'

The prattling died. Her long blue eyes lowered their lids and her mouth fell open as she seemed to search my face. Then she turned away in the bed, as if hating something, or simply impatient with herself.

'Oh, we'll see,' she said. 'Less of the past—let's talk about us now. Let's go away.'

And we began to talk of the impossibility of going away—her stocks and shares, my music manqué. Yet one day? We looked to the Spring.

But all the time I was thinking: Three. Who? When? Where? It is extraordinary how strongly these simple physical statistics, despite all our objectivity, erect their awful importance. Whatever is bleated of the superior torment of spiritual infidelity—it is when people get into the wrong bed that the pistols come out.

The solitary purposeful young women one sees

from the top of a bus! The well-dressed good-looking young women, coming from somewhere, going to somewhere, *alone*! Are they real? If so, why has one not met them? They, who are probably married or engaged or in love, appear so very available: just because they are alone.

Marie is one of these women. She perpetuates a solitary independence . . . because she lives alone. People who live alone can only be brought into perspective by an entourage, in fact by other people. So far, her only entourage is made up of Eileen and Colin, and dead Anglo-Turkish-Irish parents. One cannot take it too seriously.

Young people who live alone seem to be in transit —and so they usually are. One day sooner or later people will gobble them up. In the meantime, they are shadowy creatures. Without the short cut of an entourage—of friends acting as distorting mirrors from the sum of whose wobbled images a vaguely true picture may emerge—one finds out slowly, slowly. A gesture here, a habit there. And each discovery, rather than giving an answer, raises a further question. For instance—why should Marie always waste, say, fifteen minutes waiting to accompany someone for five minutes down the road to the Tube Station only to part in different directions? If she has so vital a need for companionship, why does she live alone? Or does living alone bring on a greater need? Or, even in today's daylit London streets, is there an inherited instinct to be escorted? Or a need to be accompanied in any case against the whole human crowd of eyes? Yet she is a capable, successful 'business lady' standing on her own small spike-heeled feet. And so on. That is how it goes. We have noticed something, discovered nothing.

Nothing? But we know there is at least a flaw in her immaculate assurance.

Other flaws: When tired out or under-the-weather, she flies to artificial means of succour. She dives into baths, perfumes, hair-sets, frictions, medicine bottles —there is almost a grandeur in her abandon at the chemists, buying left and right and centre, and certainly in the size of her bill: and in the amazing figure she cuts as from all this she rises, like a phoenix, a fine fresh bird reborn in every feather.

And charming inconsistencies. Thus, at lunchtime one day, I point out through the restaurant window a colloquy of street-sweepers, three men and their little wheeled bins come together in the shelter of a church wall for a smoke and a long talk. I smile at this leisurely scene—but say that this is where the rates go. She takes me very seriously, I am told how hard and inhuman I am. 'After all,' she says, 'they don't have much of a life.' Yet on the way back to the office, in a delicatessen shop buying cold meats for dinner, she has to wait while the white-smocked girl behind the counter completes her gossip with a regular customer. 'I suppose the shop's open?' she shouts obliquely to me. 'Aren't these working hours?' she yells.

Culture. After seeing some pictures together, we sit on the seat outside the gallery quite elevated. She has been overcome by a certain little landscape: 'Why *is* it?' she says. 'Why *that* one? Is it really so much the way it's painted—or am I half-recognising a scene I know?'

'Or does it make a pattern whose abstraction would satisfy us anyway?'

'Or even the thickness of the paint, the stroking—is it a straight sensuous pleasure?'

So we go on. But a day or so later, booked for a concert, and neither of us in a hurry to go, one of us blurts out at last: 'Poulenc. After all . . . Poulenc.'

'Plonk, plonk, plonk.'

And that is that.

We laugh, we don't go, together we have put culture in its place. High spirits, companionship and a walk on the winter streets are more than all the music in the world.

On a Sunday morning, as the local streets fill with people coming out of church or strolling towards the noon-opening pubs or both, we pause with several other passers-by to admire a little front garden sprouting in front of a terrace house.

Some of the neighbouring patches contain no more

77

than a motor-bicycle, others brandish the brown skeletons of last year's weeds. But this one is lovingly patterned with shells, rough nuggets of marble, red bricks. A statue of a giant frog painted silver squats in the centre. All shows care and artistry. But what we pause to admire most are—flowers!

During the last days, a blanket of wet warmth has stolen into our February: and now this garden's moist earth has begun to sprout aconites, snowdrops, and even a few sharp yellow and purple crocuses! Everybody has the feeling that Spring is here. We take deep breaths of damp, polluted air and feel the better for it. The flowers remain unmoved, quite brazen beneath so many eyes.

Then the door opens, and out comes the owner. She smiles so that no one need feel embarrassed, and begins busying herself on the brass doorbell, her back turned.

But the people are embarrassed, one by one they move on. For the owner, an old woman, is particularly hideous—one-eyed, with a nutcracker nose and jaw, hunchbacked, with both legs bandaged and ill.

Marie grips my arm, so that I cannot move. She is embarrassed by all this embarrassment, sees that we stick our ground. 'Poor old thing,' she whispers.

When after a few seconds, to lighten a certain tenseness in the air, I whisper that the crocuses look just like a scattering of purple Cadbury's Milk and yellow Gold Flake cartons—oh yes, and the snowdrops like torn dance programmes—I am swiftly rebuked. We are plainly on holy ground.

When finally we pass on, after a mutual smile of some intensity between the two ladies, there is a good five minutes of silence. We walk with our heads bowed.

So much beauty, Marie must be thinking, out of ugliness. . . . And I? Despite the holy strictures, my heart is loving this little act of consideration. It is infectious and warming.

'But, darling, you *must* earn more than that! I mean, your clothes, the flat . . .?'

'Not a penny.'

We are lying in bed discussing her income. It is she who has introduced the subject. Even so, it seems wrong to discuss cash so close to a body. I feel immoral and guilty. A few decades ago it would have felt immoral simply being so close to a body: conversely, discussions of cash were proper and sensible between men and women in love. Purity is like a mad white flea hopping from mind to body, body to mind throughout history.

'Then I have a small expense account.'

'Ah.'

'No, I don't fiddle it much. The point of an expense account is that it satisfies certain hoity-toity demands. It gets you into the top restaurants, theatres, and you take taxis—'

'But with the wrong people?'

'Doesn't matter, you get there. You don't feel so excluded. You taste and see. And enough of that sort of thing's as good as a—'

'Appetite comes with the eating.'

'Only the taxis. Nobody could have too many of those. But otherwise . . . besides, many of one's business friends *are* the right people. Look around and see who's friends with who—'

'Whom.'

'Very often because they're in the same line. Will you tell me the differences between two people being plopped together in similar offices and two people plopped down as neighbours in the same suburb?'

'You produce the only argument for living in London—here one may choose one's friends.'

'I wonder.'

'And I'm still wondering how you manage to make two ends meet so well.'

'Oh, economies—behind the scenes. Look at that awful old suspender-belt over there—no don't, *don't* . . . besides, I'm old-fashioned enough to allow myself sometimes to be taken out.'

'By gentlemen?'

'I wouldn't call them that.'

'Men?'

'Business men. They seem to expect goods for their money—oh, I can tell you the front steps here have known some skilful delaying actions. I think that's why they built so many little halls and glass doors.'

She seems in a happy enough mood for me to risk what all this time has been nagging inside. Very casually I say:

'Anyhow—if you've got so little, why let Colin batten on you in this way?'

Her reply is instantly defensive:

'What battening?'

'Well . . . you put him up, feed him, and I know you lent him a pound again yesterday, you said so.'

'Are you worrying about being paid back yourself?'

'That's not nice, darling.'

'Sorry.'

Silence.

We lie together a long way apart. I reach for a cigarette with the kind of muscular care fit for a tight-rope. Marie is staring at a small hummock of blanket at the end of the bed, her own toes. She might have seen a ghost. Indeed, the hummock looks like one.

At last she says: 'You've got to help your friends.'

'But is it such a help?'

'He was broke and had to eat, didn't he?'

'Hadn't he. No, seriously—wouldn't it be better to let him find his own feet the hard way? Leaning on your kindness, he'll just go on drifting.'

'But this is only tiding over until his luck changes.'

'Luck's often the result of effort. I don't expect he's bothering to put himself in the way of luck.'

'But I can't let him go hungry.'

'Why not?'

'For one thing, he'd get it from someone else. Get into bad hands perhaps.'

'Or less possessive ones?'

'That's a dirty crack.'

'Of course, it's none of my business.'

'I don't think it is.'

'Though I'm not so sure.'

'Oh?'

'No.'

'Who's being possessive now? Or are you still worrying about your old two quid?'

'In a way, yes. It makes me feel part of a long line of suckers. But I mind mostly because it's you who seems to lead the line. It's not much good really, is it? Even for him? Look at it from his point of view.'

'What's to become of him then?'

'Let him exhaust his sources of borrowing. He'll come face to face with having to *do* something. Doesn't matter what. People get temporary jobs of all kinds nowadays—from dishwashing upwards.'

'You don't know Colin. Besides, his sources are inexhaustible. Darling, he's in a pretty bad way. Look at these digs, for instance—it's bad enough, going from room to room and not paying the rent. But one day I found out something else—he often left with an eiderdown or something, and hocked it. God, I made him swear never to do it again—but you know what it is, it's as you say so *easy*, few people are going to prosecute, all the time and trouble of going to law over such a small sum. Until he happens to come across someone really angry—then he's for it, of course. So all in all, it's best to prevent him having to do that kind of thing—by helping.'

'You don't think perhaps a summons might make him sit up?'

'Jail?'

'Why not?'

'You're a nice kind of friend.'

'I simply don't see why people like him should take it easy and live off the provident, who would also like to take it easy, but don't, who settle for a share of work. As you.'

'*Like* me. Because, I suppose, he's got principles.'

'*Principles?*'

'Oh, Colin goes off the handle about a lot of things —bourgeois this and bourgeois that, toeing the line, blasted plutocrats, blasted bureaucrats, soon it'll be blasted prolocrats. . . .'

'Persecuted?'

'He gets pretty furious.'

'And so he goes and lives off other people—to be the saintly untouched one?'

'I know. It's an old story. But he does get really angry. He sits there brewing himself. He's a little mad, I think.'

'He wants to get away with an eiderdown, so he works himself into a frenzy of righteousness about the landlady being a thieving bitch and a lying old so-and-so, and so he'll show her—'

'Oh yes, *yes* I know you're right. All I say is he does *feel* it.'

'So do I feel it, I don't like a lot of things. But that doesn't mean you should pay my rent.'

'Just now. Not always.'

'Whenever things get too much. Then he's back again. But the big point, Marie, is that he's not unique. There are tens of thousands of him. Glib, easy little fake anarchists without a thought in the puss except for themselves.'

'Get back to what we do about it.'

'Do? He wants to rid the world of hypocrisy. At one go. A light task indeed! No, if that's what it is— all he can do is live up to his best precepts himself, trip up a few sinners to their faces on the way and—'

'Get trodden on. No—I meant what do *we* do about—'

'Why shouldn't he get trodden on? It's in a good cause.'

'I meant what do we do about *him?*'

'Get him a job?'

'Tried.'

'Well, let me try.'

'You?'

'I might get him to photograph a band. If he's got anything special to offer other commissions might follow.'

'Oh, darling!'

84

'Eh?'

'You couldn't *really*?'

'Well!'

'Oh, that's so sweet of you. That really is *sweet* of you, darling.'

In a twinkling—no, with a decent pause somewhere in the twinkling—her head is on my shoulder. She makes a small burrowing movement with her nose against my chest. The pause has been a kind of apology: but nothing can now remove the suspicion that a short cut to her affections leads through Colin.

Later, very casually:

'Marie?'

'Yes?'

'You're in love with Colin, whatever you say.'

'You don't understand.'

The next afternoon my doorbell rings to admit— and I mean 'admit', the threshold of a box-flat is a poor guardian, there is no doorstep between you and your visitor, he almost falls in as you open the door —to admit Colin.

Half-heartedly I begin: 'I'm supposed to be work- ing—' But the heart's other half has already stood aside to let him pass. He comes in with the look of someone who is already in a hurry to be off—his body unrelaxed, as if he were clutching invisible parcels.

'Remember that two quid you lent me the other day?' he begins. 'It's really about that.'

'Do sit down.'

We have somehow sidled into the sitting-room.

He looks suspiciously at a chair as if it were occupied, and remains standing. 'It really was most awfully good of you.'

'Oh, not at all.'

A pained look upsets his forehead. 'The fact is,' he says, now with an open stare, frankly pained, 'I can't let you have it just now.'

He looks so hurt that I have to cheer him: 'No matter. It didn't have elastic on it.'

He coughs. 'That's extraordinarily good of you.' And then he just stands looking round the room.

So there's my man! Standing there. In daylight. Do I loathe him? Or just dislike him? Neither. How much an adversary loses when he escapes from the imagination into daylight! As far as I am concerned, Colin might now be any other man. I've no real quarrel with him. There's nothing in his manner I dislike. In fact he's quite likeable—certainly to women, of course, but generally not so bad all round. I might get quite fond of him. It is only with her that the argument exists, if it exists at all.

'It's very good of you to look at it this way,' he says at last.

'Not at all.'

We are both still standing. This is rather absurd, we are too big and the room is too small. What are we waiting for?

'I've done a very silly thing,' he says.

Ah!

'I've written a bouncer.'

Now both of us stare at the toes of our shoes. As I lower my head I feel my eyebrows rising, like water trying to find its own level.

'Yes,' he says, 'and they've cottoned on. They'll be round. Trouble is these particular people have Marie's address.'

'Marie's?'

'I mean, I gave Marie's address as mine. In between moves, you see. And, of course they'll be there asking for me.'

'I'm sure Marie will protect you. It seems to be her principal métier.'

'What? No, seriously, it's her I'm worrying about. She knows my present address and she'll have to lie about that. It's not nice for her. Such a small amount, too.'

'Oh?' I said.

'A fiver. I thought possibly—'

'No.'

His whole face, attitude, stance, tone changed. His eyes twinkled, his lips twitched in a private smile, his body relaxed in sudden surety—in short, he was amused.

And I was the object of his amusement.

He stared at me, twinkling inside, removed his eyes for a moment to look pointedly about at the pictures and furniture, which suggest a mild affluence, and then returned to me.

I felt myself grow smaller and smaller.

And then I panicked and broke a silence that might finally have removed him: 'In any case,' I said, 'I haven't got it.'

He laughed:

'We're a bit tight, eh?'

A masterly double meaning—tight in the bank, tight-fisted too. And he went on twinkling, gloating, delighted. He might just as well have shouted out loud: 'What a mean little fellow he is! For a mere fiver, which he could plainly raise, he'd let Marie in for heaven knows what trouble. Or he'd let me in for a summons. He'd let anything happen but part with a little cash. Oh how dearly he loves his cash, the little man, how he loves his bourgeois little lights! Look at him—disapproving of my shameful way of living! Brrrr! Where's his mother?'

But, of course, very cleverly, he said nothing. Except, now secure in his new position, to turn the screw: 'I see your point pretty clearly. But you must admit— it's a bit of a hole I'm in? If you could even go so far as two quid, a quid even, it'd be something. I could look for the rest elsewhere.'

What does one do? I feel my lips getting thinner, my fingers longer and more crooked, I am literally being turned into a miser as I stand there! A small bowler hat forms itself on my office-whipped brow,

an umbrella reaches to take me off to the City-bound
8.20! Away from this heinous free-living, this vaga-
bond squanderer!

There are moments when tears, masquerading as
blood, mount behind the eyes. The call for physical
action is sounded. A single shattering blow in the face
—in the face, always in the face, for we are after the
personality. Anything is better than being laughed at.
Ridicule, sarcasm, irony, are great precursors of
violence.

'I'm sorry,' I say—and my voice suddenly squeaks
—'but no!'

The squeak is fortunate, its sudden shrill mouse-cry
brings me to my senses, restores the lion, and I can
add quite evenly: 'That's all, I imagine? Now—I'm a
bit busy.' And I look at the door.

Too late I see that I have to smile. The entire argument has gone on inside my head. On the face of it,
we are friends, he is my guest. So that by the time
I have stuck out some teeth, he knows that he has
struck home.

'Sorry you've been *troubled*,' is his last word, as,
every inch an officer and none a gentleman, he takes
a knowing leave.

I turn back into the flat bristling. The white teeth of
the piano, blacked like a tramp's, openly leer. The
carpet extends prickles. The pictures are eyes. To
overcome this, I allow my resentment to swell, and
invent fabulous tales of what I said to him, how with

incisive wit and disarming urbanity I polished him off
until I am the right size again.

A quarter of an hour later I rouse myself abruptly
from these invigorating dreams. Marie must be
warned.

The telephone gives me the mysterious noises of an
office—the whisper of typewriters and distant voices,
the echo of an uncarpeted room, the tolling of one
small typewriter bell, little bell lost, as if it lives in the
wire somewhere between the office and myself.

When Marie comes I tell her quickly all that has
happened. It is, of course, like speaking to a stranger:
she has answered with a telephone voice, and I can see
all that office equipment mounted behind her. She is so
quiet that when I have finished I say: 'Hello? Hello?'

'And you sent him away?' at last comes the voice,
slowly, now terribly near.

'Of course.'

'Don't you realize the man's in real trouble, issuing
a bad cheque?'

'Oh, but the story was faked from beginning to
end. He was simply counting on my feeling for you.'

The voice snapped, 'And you showed it, didn't you?'

'Marie—please . . .'

'God knows where he is now!'

'I should think he'll turn up soon enough.'

'In the meantime—you might go out and look for
him.'

'That I shall certainly not do.'

'What?'

'Please, Marie—look at it sensibly, he's just trying every trick—'

'He's helpless and you've denied him. You might at least have given him something on my account, I'd have paid you back, you needn't have worried about—'

I clapped down the receiver. It was too much. So, of course, was clapping down the receiver—and a minute later I was regretting it. Here was the kind of rough treatment I should have given Colin, yet it is she who receives it.

I sit back deflated. I am made of sham, wilful balloons that never burst. And the trouble goes deeper, they symbolize the whole unsuccess that surrounds me—the music sheets, the jazz orchestrations, the toneless little piano, the recording pay-slips of one who imagines himself something of a poet and serious composer yet refuses to suffer in the accredited fashion, to concentrate, and starve a little. I'm a fake. And like a true fake, love the commiseration of admitting it.

Later, I cross over to the window and stand for a while wedged uncomfortably between the desk and the sill, looking down from four storeys on to the small patch of street visible—in the hope that by chance Colin might pass. It is a concession to my guilt. If he did pass I could do little about it by the time I reached street level—but if I did, it would always be 'by chance'. Faces everywhere would be saved.

V

IT is a beautiful day, a free and wonderful day, a day dazzling and always to be remembered, with the sun blazing gold on puffs of pink and yellow blossom and the ground white with snow, bright white snow everywhere.

Through this magic morning Marie walks with me, hand sometimes in hand, as together we breathe in the crisp cold air and feel the sun warm on our eyes.

A fortnight has passed. All has been settled.

Colin has a job. The air has cleared. And nature itself seems to have entered the conspiracy with this blue and gold, winter-white morning of sunlight.

After my rudeness that day on the telephone, I saw Sam Paris and asked him whether he wouldn't like the Boys photographed? Sam said not on his life. However, he told me later that Bert Navarro wanted some publicity, let him flog a dead horse, let him, it's not my money, Sam said. So I went to Bert who hummed and hah'd and ran a finger up and down his enormous nose and finally said it was a good idea and thanks, but he'd manage for himself, he had a friend with a Rolliflex, but *he* knew that Les Cone wanted a picture of his Jambeaters . . . in fact, for a couple of days I talked my feet off round the offices and ended indeed with an assignment for Colin to photograph what I had

92

never imagined, the entire Edgar Kent String Orchestra. Colin was delighted. But unfortunately . . . running expenses . . . so in for a penny, I lent him a pound to buy a film for the camera which he would borrow. He took this as his due and instantly became exuberantly professional—thanking me only as an afterthought. His naïveté was engrossing, almost charming.

But when Edgar Kent's thirty tired pieces were called to a rehearsal in their dinner-jackets at two in the afternoon, Colin never turned up. Nor did he telephone, nor bother to apologize afterwards. Quite simply, he had something better to do—Eileen had found him a regular job. Her last department store was starting a photographic section with a live studio for certain publicity reasons, Eileen had managed an interview for Colin, and Colin had bluffed his way to acceptance. Meanwhile, Edgar Kent swore at me, his musicians swore about their laundry bills, and I suppose Colin and Eileen drank in celebration my pound's worth of unbought film. Neither charming nor naïve; but best, in the circumstances, to be forgotten. At least he had a job and was off our hands.

In the meantime, nature was playing less sordid tricks. A spell of extraordinary warmth, unseasonal and exciting, had brought out the blossom absurdly early—and now flowers of white plum, pink almond, yellow forsythia swarmed like butterfly clouds on the leafless winter branches. On top of this the snow fell—

gently, like a blessing, a sparkling white sugar of snow over everything. It was overwhelming, magnificent.

We were out for the whole Sunday, our destination the gardens at Kew. It was touch and go whether the sun would bring people out, or the snow keep them in. The snow, called in London 'messy', triumphed. There were only enough persons in the gardens to people it; it was ours but for a figure here and there to undesolate the glitter.

Sounds echoed wide as a childhood morning, the domed glass of the palm-house glittered a sabre-flash of sunfire back to a pale blue sky, the snow sparkled high on branches and spread wonderfully white over the lawns and meadows; and at its edges, where the black asphalt had been swept and the white crust dissolved, there was a dribble of wetness pure as spring water. Pink and yellow flowers sang out against the white. Blossoms and snow, cherry and Fujiyama—and I began to hum under my breath the obvious *One Fine Day*, and its sad drift and fall suited that longing for the past which all good weather brings, memories of virgin childhood when, for a passing first moment, one breathed freely and the small heart truly sang. And she hummed it too. She took it up instantly, and it was good to be understood so quickly.

We were, of course, in the pathetic terms of adults, children again. As we breathed in the clear air, as the chill peppered the insides of our noses, as the warmth of the sun struck our cheeks and the dazzling glittering light flew in from everywhere to blind the corners of our eyes—as with childhood, when a black frame seems to surround each brightly seen memory—so with her hand in mine the illusion of childhood grew, and I felt that if I turned, I might see beside me a very young girl's face smiling in the sun. One is almost persuaded, at such moments, that childhood really was a happy time.

Yet when I did turn, I saw of course an adult woman, no avoiding that. But I also felt a sense of relief. How to explain *that*?

Unless it was that such a morning seemed to ventilate a certain restraint that had grown up between us over the last weeks. When I had apologised for my rudeness on the telephone, she had laughed it away: 'A moment's aberration,' she said, 'it might as well have been me—I.' She had, it seemed, absolutely forgiven me. But she was not quite honest about this. When we had made love, a little after, she was neither exactly cold, nor quite absent—but carefully compliant; I was in the position of someone receiving his exact change counted out in detail, no extras given.

It continued like this. It was like making love to something indefinitely remote yet still operative— like a well-trusted lighthouse. Easy to joke . . . but at the time I worried a lot about it, wondering about all sorts of things, about frigidity, about delayed frigidity, and I remember recalling theories of frigidity, like the one that really beautiful women may not too easily lose themselves in love—they already have their attachment, the mirror: not so the mousey ones—it is the mice who make good lovers, they go in for all they're worth. And with Marie, who is a borderline case, a beautiful mouse?

However—today the bright morning seems to have melted these little coldnesses, whatever their cause. It was a morning for affirmation: and, of course, Colin was at last fixed up.

My Turk, I think—there against the snow! My nice little Turk with the blue eyes, primping along on legs like cellophane sticks above her fur boots; and higher up, a waist so thin it balances her whole small body, she hangs back on it, you can imagine the strong small furrow running up her back, and one arm swings wide as the other clutches her bag into her side.

Her nose is a little red with the cold. Her lipstick always so wet is parched; and her eyes wet. She turns and gives me a wide western smile from dry oriental lips. How much oriental? How much Turk since that old Irish mercenary forebear went to fight the Sublime Porte's wars? Mariohara—run together it sounded Polynesian, people sometimes took it for a surname.

In the palm-house she suddenly becomes serious. Confronted with an exotic flower, whose intentions are obvious, she stares fascinated at the coloured waxen flesh, epicalyx and proud pistil—and shudders. But shuddering, she reaches forward a hand to touch it. Her finger pauses a hair's breadth off the plant, hovers, draws back. 'What awful things,' she says: and her eyes say, 'How beautiful!'

So warm among the palms that we flap our coats open. The sunlight streams in, the hot air smells of iron and under-leaves; it is immediately relaxing after the crisp outside air. She catches me yawning and turns a sly eye at the winding iron staircase climbing up among the palm-trunks: 'Time to go upstairs?'

We are standing by a large Chinese rhododendron. With a quick look up and down for peaked caps we move behind massed white flowers and our mouths join in a long, longing kiss. But it is forbidden. She clings to me for a moment, clings too closely—and then looks tired and sullen, shakes her head: 'Let's go.'

We hurry to the fresh air, and breathe it in like guilty children. In a few minutes we are recovered. And this is pleasant! How can two lovers feel so pleased to be released from passion into innocence? What are we made of?

And the day passes.

The day? A succession of moments enclosed in the same dazzling glass of weather. Single moments mar-velling at anything that strikes the eye. The moment of the old man, punting himself through the snow with his stick. The moment of the two children using bright metal tins as stilts, tins held on by strings. And then the longer moment when we discovered that we had both once spent childhood holidays, long long ago, at the same seaside resort. A bond tighter than any other was formed. We shared a memory. Shingle and wet sands, breakwaters and green weed, tired early-to-bed nights with grown-up music echoing, mysterious cycle-rides into the back country, high hedges and meadows—whatever it was, we were given a present of Time. Yet what really happened when we talked of Alnwick? We must have tried to imagine each other there—but what each of us really saw was our own self. We revealed ourselves to each other by staring, quite separately, each into an old mirror. But how warming, how much closer we pounced.

Time, place—Alnwick added something substantial to my picture of her. Apart from that lonely lack of entourage, that solitary flat-living life we have talked of, Marie had a further claim to anonymity. She was part of that curious limbo lived in by people whose attitudes and thought, and sometimes even appearance, are radical and independent: she had shown herself to be free, kind, sensible—by high character she had eliminated character from her own person. One wanted stock characteristics with which to align her. Outspoken types are essential to an inexpressive, untalkative nation. But Marie fell into no easy category.

Had it been a warm and lazy day, we might have lingered on with Alnwick and the past: but as it was cold, we talked of our ambitions. I, of my unmade music: she, well—of what? She was indecisive. To be chairman of her Trust? She laughed—ridiculous, a business career for a woman was less of a career than a means to an unknown end. 'I live, and I'm independent,' she said, 'and like anything else, the work's not without interest: one wants to succeed within the limits. And, you know, *people* are involved. The clients may be no more than names and addresses, but you imagine them. And finance isn't figures—it's habits, fashions, politics.' And finally: 'Having put an end to chivalry with our emancipation, a woman must see she lives on equal, or if necessary more equal, terms.'

'But in the end?' I said.

And I could have bitten off my tongue. For the end is mostly marriage—and my own intentions loomed suddenly delicate and disloyal. I could have bitten off my head . . . the sins buzzed hungry as bees in the black hive I now hung in shame, and my heart panted the wrong role: 'Pray only give me time . . . you shall have your answer tomorrow.'

'Oh well, who knows?' says Marie, shrugging the whole question into thin air, 'who knows anything nowadays? If ever there was a time with a tremendous future—yet nothing quite to hang one's hat on, if you see . . .'

Like a dog freed from his faeces I walk faster—I want to run away from where the dirt was laid, run off all over the wonderful free park.

But no sooner has this peril been overcome than

another trap yawns before us—the great red wooden Victorian tower of the Chinese Pagoda. Into this, casually curious, we stroll. Plain boards, emptiness— a hollow wooden place echoing the slight sound of our lonely entry, two together.

Empty houses are sounding boards for personality: persons grow huge in them. Empty rooms with their bare boards invite action, like the stage of a theatre. We drew closer, arraigned before this emptiness—I smelled the fur on her hat, and her hair, and the scent she wore. She raised her eyes and her eyes looked bruised—we were in half-dark, in secrecy, and both of us knew it, and I was thinking: Would no one come? Was there time? . . . when again that same sad petu- lance, that sullen look seemed to fatten her face a little, puff it, round it out with the look of a greedy child, and then with one of the swift movements she had, the sparrow-sharp movements of a small woman, she took my arm and abruptly led me out to safety.

I could have cried for joy. She had so plainly refused because she wanted me. All her compliance during the past cool weeks seemed so obviously false compared with this opposite, this willing refusal. We were lovers again.

And it was time to go. The sun's last rays now lit up the gardens like a giant low-lying lantern, turning white of snow to pink and all the different blossoms to a mystery of lavender, lilac, mauve, deep purple. And this strange lamplight struck sideways at the branches

of trees, gilding them from underneath with a breath-
taking floodlit gold. We walked to the gates over a
carpet of rose beneath golden snakes.

A cheery chintzy café we had passed earlier had
looked too sad—and we decided against tea, and stood
for a few minutes by the bus stop. A taxi, lost in the
darkening suburb, came coasting along. Marie shot
her arm up, balancing forward on the kerb-edge as if
it were a cliff. 'Taxi!' she called. At that lonely twilit
hour, among dark brick houses etched in a winter's
steel engraving, the word rose like a cry of Greek
grief.

As we hustled in, she said: 'It's on me.'

'It's mine,' she insisted, 'I called it. And I've made
some money—I was going to buy a bestial blouse
yesterday morning. Missed it now—last day of a sale,
you know. So I've made upwards of two pounds, two
delicious pounds to spend.'

'You won't catch me investing in *your* Trust,' I said.
She gave me a sharp, delighted look: 'And if I'd
bought the blouse, worn it a few months to satisfy
your animal views, and then sold it—would I have
made two pounds?'

'You'd have been doing someone in the eye,' I said.

I was going to kiss her, but that would have been
too much like a taxi-kiss, and instead she just leant
back on my arm and, wonderfully fatigued after the
long winter day, we watched the gilded eaves and
blazing vermilion chimney-pots of London pass as

the day sank to its finish and the taxi entered among the taller metropolitan houses where we lived.

I very nearly said goodbye at her door. Somehow it seemed important to leave the glass bubble of that day intact and memorable, just as it was, no tailing off —I even began to make the excuse that I had promised to play that night, and ought to rest and change quietly—but she pulled me in, we went upstairs, and within a very few minutes were gone in each other's arms, the day and everything else locked out.

Afterwards, she said: 'Have a bath here—do *please*. I hate you to go.'

As I turned the taps, I heard her telephoning, and then she came in and poured into the bath an essence that smelled of scented wood, and set out a huge white warmed towel—and then I was left to lie back and soak my tired muscles in a soothing heaven of steam and hot water. But a moment later the front doorbell rang and I thought Hell, and looked round the room for escape. There was a kind of clinking, a few words —I thought I recognised the porter's voice—and the door shut again. Silence. And then she came in with two tall strong tumblers of whisky in her hand. 'Like some blouse?' she said.

The steam rose and we sat there with the whisky and the hot water and the towels and drank and quietly talked. A white whirling of snowflakes flashed on to the small black bathroom window, the sense of beautiful tiredness was complete.

Blue cigarette smoke curled up with the white steam and I remember thinking: That fear, that frigidity now for the moment melted, had nevertheless existed. It was fact. Once and for all, the first spontaneity of loving, the absoluteness, was finished. But something else is born in its place—we are now attached the more deeply by a need to consider each other. The big bargain is on.

It was comforting to think this. I felt grown-up again; and that, however enchanting an illusion may be, is what a grown-up person likes best.

An hour or so later, when we arrived together at the New Marlven, Belle was at the door and told me that Colin had been in and out several times asking for us.

'Looks a bit happy, got a tart with him,' Belle said.

And just then he poked his head round the door and swayed towards us, his mouth a big joyful circle, his eyes twinkling good-fellowship, and Eileen following behind with a face drawn as death.

VI

THE whole beautiful day burst like a bubble. . . I
took half a glance of pathetic hope at Marie, but
her face was wide with welcome. Old friends
met! At the first touch from outside, our new texture
of two-together had collapsed.

Of course, we all went in. We took a table near the
piano. In another ten minutes I would have to play.
Did she now consider us, perhaps, impregnable? As
settled lovers or a man and his wife may welcome a
third, against whom they can play themselves, and
pass away the time? Could I draw comfort from so
tenuous a possibility? I tried.

The club looked clean, its hair well brushed for the
evening not yet begun. The ashtrays winked with
polish and the bar glittered its altared screen of glass
bottles—the damask walls and the fringey soft
furnishings looked almost luxurious. Andrew in a
white coat was quietly cutting lemons among his
silver shakers. Only old Armitage and his hen-like
wife were in: they sat in their corner deep in one of
their interminable talks—she pecking away at him with
her pretty beak, a cockscomb of a plum-coloured hat
nodding forward each time her glassy-eyed rooster
nodded yes.

Belle served us. Colin seemed to be in high spirits:

'This is on me,' he kept saying, and when he ordered the drinks, grunted largely: 'Large ones!'

'But you can't,' I said, 'you're not a member.'

I took out a pound and nodded to Belle to get the drinks, and when she had gone Colin made a firm and fussy business of putting my pound note back in my pocket and one of his own into my empty hand—fumbling like an awkward uncle whose generosity hurts.

'A little celebration!' Colin says.

'Hooray then!' from Marie, who is sitting very erect, with an ears-back look, intent on pretending that there is nothing unusual in any of this.

Eileen has not spoken a word.

Tonight she carries a transparent plastic bag, a small museum-case in which many of her most intimate possessions are visible, powderbox, lipstick, cigarettes, and a dirty little handkerchief: it seems to speak for her, and says too much. But Eileen herself is really far from quiet. She keeps on shifting about, as if her underclothes were troubling her. Both ladies in fact, in their different ways, are properly on edge. Only Colin is at ease. Once again, as he leans back with his glass, one hears the strains of the Destiny Waltz, the rumble of howitzers, the giggle of flappers. 'His teeth flashed like a tin of Gold Flake.' I look closely for a moment at Colin's trench-hardened skin, at the amiable crows'-feet round his eyes. How are some men so uncompromisingly *manly*? Weathered, but never out in it?

'What a lovely day,' I say to my whisky, 'it's been.'

'*Has* it?' Colin laughs hugely. 'Haven't seen a lot of it myself—have we, Ei?'

'Huh,' the plastic bag replies.

'Been celebrating,' he goes on. 'In and out of little dark underground holes all day. Clubs. Pubs. Wine! Song! Very unhealthy.'

Eileen suddenly raises her face, her voice too:

'Celebrating! Celebrating *what* I'd like to know?'

'Now, now—easy does it!'

'I'll tell you what we've been celebrating,' she goes on with scorn, 'we've been drinking to the fact that Colin's got himself the ruddy sack.'

'Come now—*resigned*!'

'And got me a stinking name into the bargain. I shan't dare look them in the face again.'

Marie says slowly:

'What's this, Colin?'

He looks for a moment disconcerted. Then the eyebrows, the whole forehead, rise in deprecation: 'I could never've stayed with that bunch of crooks. A miserable salary, half what the job's worth. Expecting you to clock in like a clerk in the mornings! I'm afraid I had to tell the Lord High Staff Manager where he got off.'

'Oh, Colin!'

Explanations, recriminations. We begin, as usual, to talk round and round Colin's circumstances, Colin's past, Colin's future. This must have happened a thousand times before and will do so a thousand times in the future—but briefly, Colin has discovered this new employment to be beneath his dignity and has insulted the staff manager to the pitch of forcing his instant dismissal, a day after pay-day, with a week's extra money in lieu of notice. Somehow he has managed to suffer the indignity carefully for a week and a day, and has made two weeks' money for one week's work. 'Giving them some of their own back,' says Colin. And adds, enigmatically: 'Two can play at that game.'

What game exactly has this department store been playing? Expecting its well-paid new studio director to turn up on time in the morning?

'But Colin, thousands of men in very high executive positions are at their desks at nine.'

Colin smiles wisely. He only sees himself in one light, the boss arriving at his leisure, and ducks the question: 'At their desks doing what? Passing on price increases to their customers, thinking up lovely schemes like "free" delivery and passing on the cost...'

'Oh, *really*,' Marie says.

'You should talk,' he snaps straight at her, 'working out "safe" investment schemes knowing that money's losing its value all the time.'

'Don't be so *simple*—'

'What about electric light filaments—made to break? What about the inexhaustible match? What happened to *that*?'

'Oh God, now we're off,' Marie says. And for a moment we all sit glumly watching Colin's face work itself into a blaze of scorn. He must be a little mad. No one can get so angry about that wicked old match any more, it is taken for granted and almost comforting, like saying 'human nature' or 'original sin'.

'Anyway,' he suddenly chuckles, patting his breast pocket, 'we've come away with some of the ante.'

And he orders more drinks, and goes through the same fuss about paying for them. His generosity is confusing—it seems somehow to make an honest man of him. It confirms his disdain for counting the pennies. One forgets that the more generous he is the sooner those who would like to be generous themselves will be rescuing him again.

But I let him go on paying. There seems little point in hotting up my own standard of living to a drink every two minutes because Colin has lost his job.

'You'll be on the rocks again,' Marie says. 'Thank God at least you've got somewhere to live for a change.'

Eileen laughs sourly: 'Fat lot *you* know,' she says. She takes up a cigarette, lights it, blows out a long puff of smoke, and then stabs it out and humbly, softly, appeals to Colin.

'Couldn't you go back on Monday and apologise? Couldn't you, Colin . . . *please?*'

Colin looks down at his white knuckles, on which small tufts of black hair grow: 'Apologise?' he smiles, quite the gentleman. 'One simply doesn't do that sort of thing.'

But Marie brought him back sharply. 'You mean you've left that new room you got?'

'I only got it to be near the store. Don't want to spend the rest of my days down in *that* part of the world.'

'And now . . . ? Your bags?'

'With the porter. I hope you don't mind? I'll find somewhere, it's early yet. Meanwhile, what about the inner man—and the ladies' insides? Another?'

Once again he claps his hands. And Marie groans: 'But it's eight o'clock, and a weekend, Colin!'

'Something in what you say,' he says doubtfully. 'However . . . now where's that bloody barboy?'

I have to play, and for once I am ready for it. Anything but listen to an endless discussion as to where Colin can get a room. Round and round and round it will go endlessly—the thought presses down a lead band of boredom dull as a headache.

And indeed, as my first notes sound, softly at first, improvising up and down—no sudden chord to startle the Armitages out of their low twittering—as I play, I see that indeed I am bored again, I've not been bored since I first saw Marie, but now the old dull disfavour has descended: and this is, of course, what people like Colin finally bring in their wake. From mouths all round him will fall suggestion after suggestion, this address, that address—all to be considered, rejected, passed over as not quite right for this reason or that of Colin's taste or comfort or whatever it is. It will all be so intense, serious, earnest—and it will never stop.

Whenever I consider boredom, I am taken back to an afternoon in Brussels when I was a few years younger. It was raining. I sat in a bar well fitted with soft metals and polished woods and glass, a smartish little bar of a common kind—and watched through the window the rain stream pewter rivers off Belgian roof slates. The *patronne* was tough and pretty. So were some of the others in the bar. It was a hang-out for layabouts— oiled men with dark eyes and bow ties passed the afternoon here, talking very softly, slowly sipping a *porto* or a *liègoise*, quietly watching the girls and themselves in pink-tinted stretches of wall-mirror. Music played from a muted speaker somewhere. It was all soft-shadowed and white-faced—nobody ever seemed to speak much above a whisper or make any defined move. My own pockets were full of hard Belgian francs—yet I was infected by this place; I could think of nothing, nothing in the world worth doing. A cinema? Get a little drunk, dance? Museums and galleries and theatres . . . nothing would do. Once or twice I overheard what these scented, painted slow-afternoon drinkers were whispering to one other.

'So Gaby told him, and he said: Right, I'll allow her eighty francs on the old radio.'

'She got it at Ghent, twenty yards. It's so pretty.'

'It's not his uncle's, it's his father's.'

So even the bloom of evil was tarnished. A lot of damn shams.

And then a goodlooking woman came in, and seeing me alone, walked straight up and whispered the following proposition: That we should go to her apartment, where for a fee of three hundred *francs belges*, she was prepared to urinate over me, dressed in the costume of an Alsatian peasant. Or, if I preferred it, of a nun. 'Most of my clients prefer the Alsatian,' she said, 'it's less ordinary.'

It seemed a hard bargain either way—and that, as the rain gushed off the rooftops and the radio plushly hummed, was about all that crossed my mind. It was the kind of proposal which, one would imagine, might shock a young man, make him sit up. But not me. And that is the point I want to make—I was so dull inside that I did not even bother to begin to wonder. I was absolutely incurious. My answer? *'Non, merci.'*

That has always seemed to me an epitome of boredom. And now here is Colin bringing the same old dullness to dowse the spirited day. Colin—I think of him as I play, he has even got *me* thinking of him, and that's his trick, people like problems and he's a living crossword-puzzle, available and free at all times. Colin, I think, and his suitcases. Two cases, one containing a change of clothing, a suit with frayed sleeves, a couple of drip-dry shirts and so on. And the other case heavy with photo-Art books—a weighty affair to suggest permanence to his cavalcade of landladies. One sometimes looks for a reason for such books—here at least is one.

Perhaps it is the very nomadic nature of his equipage that has given Colin his 'weathered' look. The pavements are his desert, whose oases of goodwill may seem to shrink as the days pass but will probably sprout up elsewhere. They are possibly inexhaustible. Whenever a man is down, there is always someone to pick him up: that is the charitable truth of our times. The difference with Colin is that he expects not only to be picked up but placed afterwards on a sofa, and not any old sofa. Not for Colin that shrug of a phrase to excuse a disagreeable action: 'One's got to live.' Colin would add the word 'well'.

Yet does he? There must be intermediary stretches when his sources of charity run dry or become unavailable—people ill or away. How does he then get on? That is a mystery. It is possible that he starves a little. But he seems hardened—for if he gets acid and cynical, nevertheless he never whines. I think complaint would seem to him an inefficiency, a loss of time and a waste of emotion. As others run to the sink at the sight of dirt, Colin would keep himself immaculately clean of anxiety. He may be not unlike those old-time trappers and hunters who learned to live off the land through which they passed, and in doing so learned how to live off nothing—to starve comfortably in bad weather. With a life in so many ways based on desire, he practises non-desire with some success. One cannot help admiring this, though it seems an unnecessarily hard path to choose. That it is hard for others, too, is the real rub.

The waltz I am playing becomes a valse as Colin's features float their anachronism across my mind. Soon we'll be having a cake-walk. I must shake myself out of it . . . pep up . . . look round . . . what kind of night is this, who's come in, how fares the old New Marlven?

A glance round reveals a few regulars. The Adrians are nestled together turning over handfuls of jewellery in their minds. Leather-wristed Raoul sits sipping a sweet cocktail and glancing over the *Vogue* pattern book. A group of young men and their girls burst into occasional loud laughter. They seem to be on their way to a dance, the men in dark well-pressed suits, with white handkerchiefs set in breast-pocket triangles, and the girls sticking naked arms and shoulders out of tulle dresses that rob them of shape yet cloud them with freshness. Indeed they all look remarkably fresh —as if they lived in rarefied air under cellophane. But as with Eileen's bag, one suspects that what is so carefully insulated could not be quite so fresh. What is the newly bathed woman in evening dress saying as, with nose in air, she descends the evening staircase? 'I don't smell.'

Only two other tables are occupied. One by two upper-middle-aged business-looking gentlemen, both wearing glasses. Their lenses flash as they nod and smile. Neither will ever see the other's eyes—they can only watch each other's lips for the truth behind the truth. And at the other table there is a thin, ill-looking angular lady in a thick wool dress. She has an old battered purse, nicely filled with notes. An alcoholic—poor dear, she is a regular for three nights once a month, when her allowance comes due. At least she is now enjoying herself, and paying pleasantly for it with banknotes, as she will pay for it otherwise later. The man she is with is better dressed than she, and younger. He's her taxi-driver. Only the television sits alone and darkened, a glassy glaucous eye watching. People here do not dislike it, but they forget to turn it on.

The fizzing of siphons, the clink of glasses, bursts of laughter, and all the murmurous mumble of voices mingling with my own soft ompety-pom, which I let fade and grow loud successively, like waves eavesdropping. Bits of fluff, smoke, ash and the smell of spirits, the muzz of noise and little flickerings of light as rings flash, teeth smile, bodies and faces move— and this whole room vibrates with an all-over presence, something not quite placeable, like the bell-hum of an aircraft on a cloudy night.

It is into this blurred monotone of people together that suddenly my chords crash as loud as a door slammed open.

Everybody jumps, my every white-knuckled finger stiff as a drumstick has slammed down its note . . .

and what has happened is like an episode in a very old film, the longest double-take in history, taking up the time of two waltzes and three foxtrots for me to realise that Colin may have to stay at Marie's tonight!

I make a coda of the chord, and go over to the table. They are still at it.

'Dorset Square,' Marie says. 'Isn't there a place ...'

Colin laughs: 'Don't be silly. I've had it there.'

'You mean *they*'ve had it,' Eileen says.

Colin shakes his head sadly at her: 'Why do you live at Walthamstow? Why do I have a girl who lives at Walthamstow with her mother?'

Then he plunges straight back into the gravity of his predicament. Working his jaw as though it holds a pipe he says: 'There's Jimmy Bradshaw and his missus in Islington—they've got a room to let. But, you know, it's a bit far out for me.'

Quite seriously the two ladies agree that Islington is too inconvenient for Colin.

Then Eileen raises her eyebrows and looks unhappily to left and right as if she has lost something. What she has lost turns out to be her understanding.

'I can't understand,' she says, 'I can't *understand* why you don't go back near where you just settled yourself. Knightsbridge seems good enough for *some* people.'

'And *you* can't understand,' Colin sighs, 'how there are other people who can't *bear* living South of the Park. All that smart jolly I'm Rightness ... oh no.'

This too is accepted! Colin cannot live South of the Park! It is extraordinary to see Marie nod seriously at this.

It had to be stopped. They were running out of suggestions, and Marie would soon have had to put the usual last solution. I walked over to the Adrians and pressed them to come and have a drink. They were pleasant, amiable people. They would serve to change the subject.

But they are too amiable by far. Levantine quickness catches the gist of the last few words spoken as they arrive; Levantine sentiment is touched at the idea of a man with no roof to his head. Levantine horse-sense tells them to wait and watch.

'And on this snowy night, too!' Myra moans.

'At a week-end!' agrees Otto, shaking his head.

Marie smiles a knowing sideways smile, her dark blue eyes deep with secrets. Eileen gives a single, quite open sniff of contempt. Only Colin does not seem to mind. He flashes his gold tooth—which I am sure the Adrians take instantly to their hearts—in a charming smile, and, strong weathered man of action, laughs:

'It'll all come out in the wash. Meanwhile—what are we having?'

And another of his hard-earned notes flutters on to the table.

Just then Marie seems to lose patience and takes the plunge. 'Well, you'd better come and sleep on my floor,' she says, 'and have done with it.'

And there was my voice saying like a sudden high bird-cry: 'No!'

I must have spoken with some violence—for now they all stop talking and look at me in a big empty balloon of silence.

'No,' I repeat, a little lower, thinking hard for a reason—for I can hardly say that I'm hoping to sleep there myself and not on the floor. 'No,' I say, 'he *can't* sleep on a floor.' And: 'Out of the question,' I add, still less convincingly. I suddenly suspect that not only can he sleep on a floor but that duckboards are his natural habitat.

But Colin, of course, has caught on. His eyes twinkle with amusement, black crows'-feet of twinkle feather the corners of his eyes, giving him a hairier look. He gives me a wink, a man-to-man connivance. It is too much. I could wish him on her floor forever to escape such a wink. 'I've been in the same boat, old chap,' he means to say. Indeed! Just any boat? Or *her* boat?

But before Colin can say anything to substantiate his wink, Otto has put his head to one side and is nodding benignly to his little wife: 'I think we could find a corner, Myra—a bed, too, couldn't we?'

'For the night, yes,' nods Myra, smiling as if some beautiful dream has come true, a prodigal returned: yet careful to cut down the fatted calf to one night.

'We've a small spare room, nothing much,' Otto says, deprecating his house, 'if you'd accept it.'

They both lean forward, beaming. With their melon mouths, short fat noses, and shining plumage, they look like two charming affable budgerigars.

Colin pretends a surprised smile. But his eyes are busy adding things up, you can almost see them clicking: 'We-ell . . . well . . . that's most awfully good of you . . . but really . . . .'

He sees that these Adrians are generous and kind people; and he knows that there exists among people who live in blocks of flats and share local clubs a kind of camaraderie. This is partly due to the myth that all transport stops at midnight, partly due to the 'local' feeling that splits a metropolis as large as London into villages. Our mechanised civilisation has brought us right back to the open-house days before there were any machines at all. Once the too open road, now the too full honeycomb—life has come full circle, and we put each other up again. All this Colin knows well. And he knows that the Adrians are friends of mine, who would know Marie by now—and that therefore introductions are unnecessary.

But Marie was shaking her head hard at him: 'I'm sure my floor'd be easier—just for the night . . . and, after all, your things are downstairs in the hall . . .'

She is plainly worried. And suddenly I am too, as I remember Colin's hand slipping that silver pot into his pocket. But she is also so plainly possessive of him that I get possessive too, somebody has to suffer—and I can always put things right with the Adrians later. I loudly insist over her head that a bed is a bed, a floor a floor, and again Colin gives me his disagreeable wink. Only the Adrians remain at ease, thinking these protestations part of a polite acceptance ritual. And finally Colin agrees to stay with them.

As a voice above me says: 'Ain't you gonna play s'more, fellah?'

It is a young man I have never seen before, a boy almost too young to be in a bar. His head sags like a pale knob of bone on a neck too thin to hold it. He wears exaggerated clothes, and a special sort of hairdress like a hedgehog's. He hunches his shoulders up to make them bigger. His eyes are dull as dead fish-scales. He grits his mouth thin as if he wants to be sick.

'In a moment,' I tell him. His tone has been really insolent, but one dismisses a lot as youth.

'Not too long then, fellah,' he says, still fixing me with his fishy dead eyes.

Behind him then, I was startled to see a kind of twin—but he was only another youth in the same cut of clothes. And then I saw that there were six or seven others standing at the bar or lounging legs stretched out from the tables. I caught Belle's eye and she gave me a hopeless shrug across the room—as if this sudden phenomenon was beyond her.

'My,' I said to Marie, ignoring the young man, who still stood there, looking down at me, 'we've got company tonight.'

'You have,' said the boy sadly, 'you certainly have.'

And he walked away, at a conscious stiff-legged strolling pace, to the bar. There he said something to the others, and they all looked my way and shook their heads —again sadly, as if I were in a very bad way indeed.

'Who on earth are they?' asked Marie.

'Never seen them before,' I said, 'and I don't ever want to again.'

We watched them for a moment. Every glance or gesture was carefully aggressive. They stuck out their legs so that Andrew carrying a tray of drinks had to circle round to save tripping—and watched him silently as he did so. One leaned over and took a tray of chips off someone else's table—unsmiling, pointedly unapologetic. Another at the bar began flipping olive stones at the bottles. Belle told him to stop. He apologised with an exaggerated bow and flipped another stone straight away. His companion gave a high cat-laugh. Belle turned her back. But she looked worried.

'They should be put across their mommas' knees,' Otto Adrian said, 'and given a good slapping. Look, Myra—look at that coat he's got on!'

Eileen seemed anxious: 'I wouldn't try it, Mr. Adrian. You don't want to get mixed up with that kind—I had a friend they properly did up . . . fish-hooks, it was.'

'Fish-hooks?'

'Sew them in their sleeves. Then rip your cheek off, horrible mess.' Eileen suddenly looked vicious, her eyes went quite dark remembering something: 'I'd like to do one of the ignorant little sods for that,' she said, not moving her lips.

'Oh, most of them just show off,' I said. 'It's natural enough at that age. They're not all dangerous.'

'Yes, and how do you tell which is which?'

Belle had come up. She was biting the end of the nail on her little finger, palm outwards—a badly worried sign.

'Why on earth did you let them in?' I asked.

'One of them,' Belle said, 'became a member a few nights ago. I must've been mad. He was quieter dressed. I didn't know he had so many friends, good God. And now for heaven's sake play something to keep them quiet.'

'Will it?'

'Great music-lovers, I thought.'

'You know,' Otto said, 'you can turn music on a bit too quick nowadays. You can turn on luxury too—beautiful dresses, wonderful rooms—see them at the cinema, on television; they're seeing all these things all the time, *almost* touching them and it looks as if everyone else but them lives like that. Not separate, as in the old days.'

'Look, Mr. Philosopher,' Belle snapped, 'that may be. But right now I don't want my club broken up.'

'Anyhow, it's not so unusual,' Colin said. 'There's always been gangs and they've always been dressing up.'

121

'For God's sake *play* something,' said Belle.

I got up. It had been a mistake to talk about them so openly. They knew they were being discussed, and now, as I went to the piano, saw that their orders had been obeyed. You could almost feel them spreading themselves. So I began to play the dimity notes of *Humoresque* to put them back a little.

Of course, it did not work. The common quality of all these young men is their watchfulness. They sit and watch everything with dull dislike. This gives them that famous 'pinched' look. As my tinkling established itself, one of them sauntered across, hands in pockets, chin down, and stood above me. He simply stated, as an order, the name of a disc-hit. Apart from this plain rudeness, a pianist's biggest bugbear is to be asked for another tune when he is already playing—so I gritted my teeth and tried to close my ears. He nudged my right arm off the notes with his elbow and said simply: 'Mush.' And repeated, louder, his request.

'Keep your blasted hands to yourself,' I said. 'Who the hell do you think you are?'

He raised his eyebrows. 'Yeh?' he said, and beckoned with his head to the others. Slowly they came over, all of them, strolling, slowly massing round the piano.

'The customers,' said the first one, 'don't like your mush.'

I went on playing, but now looked up and around at these dead young faces. Bicycle-chains, little nicks of razor in the finger-nails, I thought.

'What customers?' I said.

Belle had come up: 'What's all this?' she said.

'You keep out of this, lady,' one of them said.

Belle's shoulders went up, spots of red flushed round the rouge on her cheeks. 'I'll thank you to know this is *my* club and—'

One of them pushed her with his shoulder: 'Just keep that big pretty puss out of this,' he said, and at the same time another edged round the side of the piano, caught hold of the lid and brought it smashing down on my fingers.

It was a long second of pain, the room went grey, hundred of mouths around me seemed to open and a long leering sound of laughter wailed out as another of them kept the lid held down trapping my fingers by the second bone-joint, and Belle reached her arm back and caught the one who had pushed her a flathand slap across the face: while the other little thug, holding the lid, pretended to ease himself round to sit on it—which would snap the bones. I just had to sit there waiting for it, the rim of hard wood locking the knuckles, both hands pinioned, no chance whatever. And the boy stood there poised to come down, and looked with a hard glint of love at me—when Belle saw and caught at his lapel and overbalanced him and I squeezed my fingers out.

As I stood up and raised them they hung in front of me not like hands but white fins, they looked dead and smashed and they felt numb, they hurt yet felt

too numb to hurt at the same time. I flapped one sideways—and one of the bastards caught hold of it:
'Shake a paw,' he said, squeezing and pumping. 'Good
doggie.'

I simply let him do it. All this had taken a few long
exaggerated seconds—and it seemed now in the same
seconds, without pause, that there came from the end
of the room by the bar a kind of bellow, hoarse and
deep as a drum: 'Hey!'

And Raoul came striding down at us, his brown
voice rumbling deep as a Spaniard's, and in either hand
a bottle grasped by the belly. Even in that second,
standing foolish and helpless, I saw that one was
French Vermouth and the other Campari bitters.

He came up very suddenly, very big. They all
turned. It was like the moment when a flash of
lightning fixes a room, everything held for a long
moment bright as a dream—Raoul with his moun-
tainous grey body and his cropped head and the big
bottles raised in either hand, and picking exactly on
one youngster who stuck out as their leader, grinning
wide at this young man as with a huge laugh he brought
down both bottles on the piano top smashing them off
at the necks so that he then held up the jagged sharp
ends wide and dangerous in either hand.

'Now,' he roared, 'who wants it? You?'

The boy kept a straight face—but his voice came
high: 'Who you getting at? Who you—'

Raoul cut him short: 'Beat it the lot of you', he

bellowed, 'or I'll cut your pasty faces to ribbons!' And he waved the bottles high and did a side-to-side little jig that at another time might have seemed funny but now looked truly terrible, a big man shifting his weight, legs astride, and a mad roll in his eyes and his tongue stuck out panting.

Vermouth dripping everywhere, on the piano, on me, on all the wide boys' excessive suits. They had all moved back, none distinguished from the other, like folds of a curtain drawn away. Only the leader kept his ground. He was white as paper and seemed to be gritting himself to stand there—but at last he too moved, but slowly, trying to stroll and giving a scornful toss of his head.

But he kept his eye on Raoul—ready to run for it. For a moment the whole club held itself in absolute quiet.

And then somebody knocked a glass to the floor and it sounded like a window smashing, and the proud leader shot forward like a rabbit, running low on bent knees and weaving to the door. The others raced for it too, they all got to the opening at once and it looked like a whole cloakroom of coats thrashing to get through—as the moment broke and everyone burst out laughing at once. Raoul bellowed a last word to keep them going, and began beating the bottles hard down on the top of the piano.

Belle was the first to regain herself: 'Hey, my Joanna!' she yelled, and everyone laughed more, but it was uneasy laughter, and then Raoul stopped banging and everyone came round to slap him on the back. Marie was rubbing my hands and bringing them back to life—and the pain with it—and then I saw the sweat on Raoul's forehead, a real dew round the edge of his cropped hairs, and heard him mutter above the congratulations: 'Stop it, for heaven's sake. I've never been so scared in all my life. That lot could have slaughtered me.'

'You?' someone laughed.

He turned on them quite savagely: 'Eight of the little swine. You don't know what they can do. Not all bullies are cowards, either, don't give me that old guff—I just surprised 'em.'

Marie was soothing at my fingers, 'How are they, how are they?' she kept saying. Belle started mopping up the vermouth and Campari, and the bar began a first-rate trade. 'One emergency,' I whispered, 'when the brave band didn't strike up.'

'Can you play all right? Do they move?' Marie said. I sat down and tried. It was painful, the ivory looked hard and sickened me, but the best thing was to strike a few chords and try to get back to normal. The air was too highly charged. It was like the end of an air-raid, when people drink and talk too nervously, fear and anger exhausting itself in sudden wild friendliness —so that now, for instance, Colin and the Adrians were bound much closer together by disaster averted, he was no longer a stranger at all.

Marie raised her eyes from the keyboard and saw them talking together and laughing like old friends—and concern for my fingers quickly changed to the old grey worry for Colin, little muscles stiffened under the skin of her face and for a moment her beauty left her, she looked plain and weary.

I found my fingers searching into the air of *One Fine Day*. I meant it to sound forlorn, our own day seemed so long ago, and she turned and smiled down at me, and stroked my hair—but after a second her hand casually came to rest and she was looking back at the bar.

'Come off it,' I said, 'he's in good hands.'

She looked down at me, suddenly scornful: 'Good hands!' she said, forgetting my own as she said it. 'I'm not thinking of him, I'm thinking of *them*. He'll be there for days. You're a fool, just when I—'

I cut in loud, losing my temper.

'You *are* thinking of him. You're worrying about his getting a bad name. You can't bear him out of your sight.' I began to blaze, caught in the nervous aftermath like all the others: furious too, about my own forgotten hands.

'Oh?' she said. 'You're butting in rather, aren't you?'

'Butting in?'

'If I decide to put Colin up on the floor—'

'The divan.'

'Oh the divan then . . . it's my business, isn't it? Why should you take it on yourself to object?'

'I should have thought that was pretty plain.'

And then, poised dangerously, like a man on a cliff wishing to throw himself over, knowing the danger and plunging: 'If it was the divan.'

'What do you mean?' she said very slowly.

'Nothing,' I said, terrified.

'I know exactly what you mean,' she said, and her eyelids were down, and her breast rose and fell quickly. She looked vicious and cruel. 'Well, if you want to know, I've never slept with him. But I would have done. Only he didn't want me.'

VII

AGLORIOUS morning again, gold-brown ash-flowers from the autumn gleaming like plush against the snow, snowlight from outside flooding the room white, all a glory to wake to. But still half-asleep, one knows that something is wrong . . .

And memory descends like a hammer, cold lead fills the stomach, the day is doomed. Last night, to demonstrate my terrible unconcern for what she said, I had played the brightest jazz in the world for an hour after. Then we had left the club separately. I had let her see herself home. And that thing she had said! My mind snaps shut as I begin to lick over this tasty wound with the lobe of my aching brain. But life leaves little time for such luxuries. In less than an hour I have to accompany a glee-singers' special recording, a dozen lusty medical students at some tom-tiddler's ho-ro nonsense. Into the bathroom for my dreadful toilet. Bath, teeth, shave and all the rest of it, every day of a lifetime. Does one keep one's mind similarly clean?

White lather against yellowing teeth—and another reflection: Am I deceived by a phantom? 'She *would* have had him.' Does this mean that she has, from her point of view, in her mind's eye view, given herself to him?

I am in the desperate quandary of a suicide choosing
between two equally convenient poisons. First, regret
that Colin had not slept with her—for if it was true
that he had refused her, then the chip to our vanity
was deep indeed. Secondly, a shifty relief that whatever the circumstances, it had not happened.

Suppose you were Bey for a day—I say, wagging
my razor at the glass—and could order it this way or
that, how would you decide? But in any case—had
it not already happened by not happening?

The studio manager calls me into the sound-room
to hear the voice balance, and I tell him: Yes I think
Froggy Would a-Wooing Go is doing very nicely.
Between us lies the wonderful smooth toffee-cream of
a wax disc and above it the needle which will make
an incision once and for all time on that particular
surface. Okay? says the manager seeing me look at the
wax. But I am thinking of other needles, other sur-
faces, and as I return to the studio, nauseated by the
thought of Colin's searching hands, the proposition
occurs: Well, why not Colin, if it had to be someone?
Altogether—what kind of man would I rather be
deceived by, if deceived I must be? By someone
similar to myself? By someone I look up to? Or by
someone who looks up to me? By him who I would
like to be, by him who is like me, or by him who likes
me? *With a rowley powley gammon and spinach . . . .*
Twelve faces stand in a crescent pumping out full-

throated song, stern and jolly, *Rowley Powley* fierce
and rolling as a Russian anthem. A frightening sound
indeed, a sound of fury. And as I play, bruised fingers
aching at every thump, I get angry too—and pass the
time by thinking all the worst things I can about her.
I pick hard on little mannerisms, whose very humanity
I might at another time find charming. The rejection
principle. Sour grapes. Run her down and run off.

'Where's my bag? Where's my bag?' she says before
leaving a room. What a come-down for an intelli-
gently reserved woman! Thinking with her lips, like
all the rest of them.

A Froggy would a-wooing go

My viper's tongue, cleft like a mind into two, licks
over occasional phrases. Those absolutes: 'You *never*
(do this or that)' . . . or 'You *always* etc. . . .' Ha!

Repetitions: After making a point, she takes a
breath, says 'No—but don't you see?' and makes her
point all over again.

And a splendid one, when she can't get away with
something: 'I can't say *anything* to you these days!'
Fishwife!

The mouse has married the bumble-bee
Pipe, cat—dance, mouse

Heads are bobbing like bottles on the choppy sea
of this new song. And I bow my own face as I
smirk: The Face at the Dressing-Table! Leaning

forward to the mirror, she flexes her ears and temples
back to make the eyes more oblique and out pout the
lips into a terrible big ballooning kiss, something a
lower order of animal would prefer to keep beneath a
tail. A wistful look overtakes the whole face. Is she
looking at herself? or at the ribbon of an old dance-
programme?

Certainly not at herself. What with all this going
on, she is the only one who has never, never seen
herself. She has not the slightest idea what she really
looks like. There is the game of catching her out at
restaurants: Who is that in the mirror wearing a dress
like mine? The look of startled half-recognition! The
half-pout! The Pout! Why, it's *me*!

There was an owl lived in an oak,
Wisky, wasky, weedle

Moments, too, of the greatest beauty—her profile
staring into space. Lips tenderly at rest, eyes lost in
dreams distant as the sunset clouds . . . breathlessly
beautiful, rare, mysterious . . . '*One* day,' she says, 'I
suppose I'll get those curtains washed.'

Wisky, wasky, weedle

And what a fine actor is that face!

Watch it take on *real assumed* pain as it sympathises.
Watch it poise itself to kill before entering a room.
Yet there are times when even so adroit an affair as this
face, this beautiful multiple signal-box, marvel of

science, eighth wonder of the world, seems to get beyond control. Peering at a baby, for instance, one would think the extra large smile overdone. But it is not. It is simply baring its teeth, it wants to eat the baby.

> *A gunner chanced to come that way,*
> *Wisky, wasky, weedle*

Her need for what she calls Sympathy—a means to call attention to herself. Symptom of a mysterious series of infantile cycles. When do these tidal fluxes occur? With the moon? With other periodicities? A capacity for stirring up trouble, for worrying when things are going well—about Colin, for instance.

> *Weedle!*

CUT! The lights click dead, the singers relax, it is time for coffee and I rush to telephone my love.

'Darling, *darling*, I'm so terribly, terribly sorry about last night!'

But instead of this that I long to say, I mumble stiffly: 'Hello. About last night . . . we seemed to miss each other . . .'

Again her voice sounds terribly near. I catch myself looking round the box for her.

'Look, I can't talk now . . . between meetings, you know,' it says.

'Tonight? Could we see each other tonight?'

A pause. Very short. A pause when she is in a hurry?

'All right.'

'Call for you? Six, six-thirty?'

'Six-thirty then. Bye.'

'Oh, *darling*!' At last the right sound has come out of me.

'Bye.'

By six o'clock any feelings of joyful anticipation have faltered . . . in half-an-hour I must confront this lovely monster, who has prepared heaven knows what further torments. She will be angry, cold, sullen. She will feel guilty and pay me out for what she has said.

The snow has stayed. As I walk round to her, steeling myself, the local Georgian streets look pretty and soft as a dozen Christmas cards. My nose is pleasantly cold, my heart hot and woolly, my goloshes a galumphing nursery joke—it is all too cosy: I slink round the yellow circles of the street-lamps, and look for support from the hard black sky twinkling its cold crystals high above.

I need not have worried.

She greets me with a fine old smile, as if nothing at all has happened. There she stands, her small moulded face golden against a white bath-robe, blue eyes smiling and saying I must feel cold, come in quick!

My heart bounds high with the helpless pang it always feels at the simple sight and sound of her. We kiss. Then she is pushing me away and hopping into the bedroom with a 'Won't be five seconds! Have a drink—on the table there. I'll be ready before you've had it!'

Ready? Ready for what? No arrangements have been made . . . however, with the taste of her still on my lips I go over and find the remains of the whisky. Whisky whasky wheedle, I hum, and cleverly think to myself: 'Of course, since it was *she* who said that thing, it's nothing to her—she's wiped it clean off the slate.'

A shout from the bedroom. 'You don't have to play tonight, do you?'

'No.'

'Good—then could we do a cinema? There's a thing at the Curzon. We could get something at a coffee-bar first?'

A cinema? This was a dark and talkless way to spend the evening?

A good thing too. We were both so bright and brittle in the coffee bar, burning our fingers on the plastic cuphandles and talking of anything, everything but the previous night, that it was a real relief to get into the dark and the quiet of the cinema.

Did we imagine that sleeping dogs might lie? A fine hope! In the middle of the night they rose up and snarled all around us. It was my fault. After making a kind of love, when we were lying together sleepless and sadly distant in the dark, I suddenly gave up and whispered: 'Is anything the matter?'

Over and over I had stopped myself, but I was

abruptly too tired to be dishonest and out it came: 'Is anything the matter?'

A pause. Then a simulation of surprise, in a very clear voice: 'The matter? No.'

We were lying loosely together, embraced at arm's length: now her arm under my neck flinched, pulled a fraction away—then stopped very still.

'Of course there's something the matter,' I said. 'You feel altogether different.'

'Oh, do I?'

'What is it, darling?'

'Why *me* all the time? Why shouldn't it be you who's different?'

By this time she was sitting up.

'If you want to know,' she added, 'you've been behaving like—like some kind of mad diplomat all the evening.'

'Mad diplomat?'

'You've been jolly polite and jolly smiling and oh —jolly frightfully jolly. It sets a girl's teeth on edge, not at all like a decent tired hunched-up young man— it's like going out with a grinning film ape.'

'A film ape?'

'And suppose—just suppose I was feeling a bit off, tired or something . . . can't one have a mood any more?'

'Of course you can have a mood—'

'Aren't you taking a bit too much on your shoulders these days? Dictating my moods, my level of behaviour—dictating who should sleep here and who shouldn't . . .'

'Oh God.'

'I may have given myself to you, but I haven't exactly signed over the lease of the flat into the bargain,' she shouted. 'We aren't exactly married, are we?'

I leapt from the bed, and stood quivering in the dark.

'Colin again!' I hissed.

We began to shout roundly at each other—but keeping both our voices curiously lowered against the dark.

You get in the most absurd state about the man! I quietly yelled. That's my business, she shot back, he's a friend and needs help. Oh? I rasped. What help—a tenner a week subscribed by a sorority of sieve-headed suckers? She: Oh! Me: That's just what you are. She: You're just hard and mean! Me: Who's mean? What do you think you said to me last night, wasn't that mean enough? She: That's what you get for not minding your own business. Me: You *are* my business. She: I'm not. Me: And I'm not hard and mean, it's only Colin makes it seem like that. She: You've no charity! Me: Who's got no charity? . . .

Round and round and round in the dark. But the dark was impossible, you need faces to have a row— and at the height of it our hands met on the light switch, flicked it on and drew back bitten.

We faced each other in bright sudden light. We were both stark naked. For a second we looked at each other, stamping like blanched savages, then ran for protection.

'No charity indeed!' I stormed, struggling into my trousers. 'What do you take me for—a bloody Assistance Board?'

'No I do not, but you men, you're all—'

'The Same!' I shouted. 'You don't seem to realise we have to keep things in some order.'

'Bloody regulations are a vice with you.'

'Huh! No woman ever made a bed properly!'

Silence. Her mouth fell open:

'No woman ever *what*?'

'Made a bed properly!' I roared.

And began to rant at the top of my voice: 'If men are bound by regulations and vision, women are bound by the everyday things around them. Men hunters, women keeping the cave straight. That's natural, that's all right—cave's got to be kept straight, gets out of order too easily . . . but what does Mrs. Housewife do, she soon makes a fetish of straightness and when she makes a bed all she thinks of is tidiness, tidiness, tidiness, keep it neat at all costs, and never *never*'—I raised my voice—'does she leave room for the feet to move about, the male foot is a foot in length and doesn't want to be bound down like a mummy, but the female—who is incidentally a foot shorter in any case, I don't mean her feet are shorter, I mean *she's* a foot

shorter—the female can't stand the look of a made
... bed ... bagging ...' and my lips were moving
slower and I felt more and more absurd as we stood
and glared at each other—when, thank Heaven, we
both broke out laughing.

But it was not settled as easily as that.

'You and Colin,' I said, 'where did it happen?'

'You mean where didn't it happen?'

Her hair was over her face, it was in her teeth as
she bared them in a consciously cruel, malicious smile.
'Here!' she said, triumphantly.

I looked down at our bed. 'When?'

I think then she saw how much she had hurt—and
hurried to add kindly: 'Oh, years ago. He was drunk
anyhow.'

'So that was it—he couldn't do anything.'

'Oh, I don't know, it's all so long ago—anyhow it
didn't mean anything ...'

'Still—you must have been making love.'

'It was after a party.'

'What difference does that make?'

'Don't you see—it was nothing. And nothing happened. It means nothing to me.'

'But it does to me.'

'How can it? When it's you who's got me and he
hasn't and I've forgotten?'

'For God's sake—haven't you ever been in love?'

'Yes,' she said more quietly.

All the argument and hardness left her, as she put

her arm in mine, linking it as if we were going for a walk. 'Yes, I am,' she said.

Was it not too perfectly done? The hopeless little pang came again, a wetness gulped up into my throat, I loved her back with all my heart. But I still wondered . . . and I hit back to test her: 'One day I'll tell you about Greta.'

Her eyes opened wide and sharp: 'Greta? Who's Greta?'

'A girl,' I said, 'I used to know.'

She pulled me down sitting on the bed, and turned me round and faced me squarely: 'Now come on, what Greta? Who's this Greta?'

Her eyes were bright with amusement, mischief, and above all a kind of avarice.

So my bitchy little test had an affirmative result! But as I recounted what I had almost forgotten under the glaring search of her interest, Greta began to sound very dull indeed, and I found myself having to embroider the girl no end: lie after lie I told, white lies to blacken the past, all in the name of present virtue, our love.

Tuesday was not one of my playing nights, but I went into the New Marlven particularly to see the Adrians and find out whether Colin was still staying with them.

It was definitely a move behind Marie's back—she was working late. From her point of view I would be 'poking my nose in', and from mine I was acting slyly and dishonestly after our mutual ventilation of the previous evening. Nervous as an eel, I marked guilty time with the picture of the drinking cardinals and our enormous Raoul—who that evening was actually knitting: 'To seek pleasure is a fool's game, to take it a wise man's,' he grated in explanation in his horny deep voice—until at last the two little polished Adrians arrived, and after much beating about the bush I was able to ask them, casually, about Colin.

But it was quite all right. He had already left them.

'Oh, he did stay a couple of nights,' Otto smiled. 'He gave us the key back early this morning. Nice fellow.'

'Oh yes.'

'He's very excited about his new job,' Myra said.

'Job?'

Otto said: 'Yes, and it shows how mistaken one can be. When he lost the other job, I was the first to say to myself, I said: There's a fool. He insults his boss. The biggest reason for a boss to be a boss is more than money, it's power. Call it "position". Insult *that* and the apple cart goes up. So with your Colin.' He paused, and shook his head. 'And what happens? Now he says he did it on purpose! And straightaway goes to a rival firm, tells them he *had* to get out, the business was run so wrong, which is just what a rival loves to hear, and the long and short of it is he gets taken on by the rival on better terms even.'

'Good heavens.'

'Why good heavens? That boy's obviously a worker.'

I needed air after this and left for a trudge in the snow. It was infuriating that Colin had come out so glibly on top, but in another way I was overjoyed to see him settled again. Marie would be once more at ease.

But I was not yet easy with her.

It was freezing hard. Old footsteps had been frozen into hard ridges, sudden glassy puddles from the day's thaw sent the feet slithering in comic directions, icicles hung from the gutters like rows of white drinking-horns, the stars were iced, rime glittered a powdered tinsel on the iron of lamp standards.

To all this I cried aloud: 'But did she ever *show* him that she wanted him? Does he know? Did she give him even *one* glance, one illuminating message of welcome, so that forever afterwards he can carry away the certainty that he could have possessed her, had he wished to take the trouble?'

Both my feet shot forward and I landed heavily on the ice, a wintry pierrot among the icicle-horns. Horns? Surely no cornutation if this had happened *before* I had ever met Marie? Yet what have the years to do with it? It's the same body. 'The moment when space meets time', I hiss at the snow: and the night icily nods.

No love affair ever stays still, it is a foolish

man who thinks he can lie back on the laurel-strewn
bed.

But during the next days a kind of peace did indeed
seem to descend. Colin was settled and gone and
thoughts of jealousy receded with him: in this calmer
climate, Marie seemed to be quite mine again, and I
all the more securely hers.

It was still fine winter weather, ice-blue days when
the town glittered like a coloured photograph. Snow
always lifts London clear out of its murk. White
houses become cream, cream houses yellow against the
snow's pure white; brown brick softens to bear-fur,
red pillar-boxes blaze deeply; chimney-smoke rises
yellow-grey on a windless air and the thin winter
branches of the trees in the park engrave the pigeon
sky like a printed score of music—particularly one
giant plane-tree, whose round black bobble-seeds
among the stave-branches looked like a spangling of
notes you could have played.

Among the keen winter smells—the restaurant whiff
of roasting meat over snow, the passing of scent and
cigar-smoke rich against frost—there came to me one
of the best of all winter smells, a kind of private
no-smell, the beginning of a cold in the nose. Immediate associations of blankets, balsams steaming, bed-
bound insulation from the rest of the world! And a
light feverish inebriation.

Muffled in my electric flat, I sat like a human eiderdown with the thoughts rising and falling like a thick

sea of feathers. It was a time of recession and assess-
ment—and often there came to me an echo of Marie's
words: 'We aren't exactly married.'

For a woman particularly, a love affair must move
in some direction: either towards the accepted condition of marriage, or at least to a statement of non-
marriage, a definition of living together or apart and
on what conditions—to say a thing is sometimes to
make it. Otherwise the thing drifts in a vacuum,
uneasily unlimited.

But who marries whom? How do you recognise
your ineluctable destiny? People are being married all
over the place, all the time. They cannot all have
searched the earth and found finally the Only-One-
in-the-World—there isn't the transport. One is
reminded of the old saying of the bullet with one's
name on it. And if one's name is Smith? No, people do
not fall in love with a unique fatality; one falls in love
with someone temporarily suitable. Loyalty, trust,
affection—the unique things—come afterwards. Love
sets the harder the cooler it gets . . . so how on this
earth can you judge?

A risky business.

There's always a thumping sweet American in
Arkansas of whom you will never see or hear, and
who would do equally well—and for whom, let's
face it, you would feel the same hopeless little
pang.

However—it is, after all, not so much for you to

make a move, the move will make itself: the stranger
inside you will do the work.

But first—a word with the stranger? How about the
Colin situation? How about marrying not only a
woman, but her parasite too—her genial great tape-
worm with its smart little moustache? Is the parasite
temporary or permanent? Has the parasite even—
and this is a biologically sound, if long, shot—his
hidden uses? After all—he has provided us with the
quickening of jealousy, he has proved to me that she
is kind and charitable at some cost to herself, and he
has made us quarrel, and anger is at least a thermometer of feeling. Ought we to keep him?

No answer. And whether an artificial stimulus like
a quarrel, or jealousy, or even a holiday has any real
value is hard to say. Doing is easier than saying . . .
and then the drifting thought of Holiday rang its bell,
clean and bright, in my muffled wanderings . . . a
holiday was just the thing? She had said she had a
week off soon? And I could make the time free? Then
we would go away together!

It would be movement, if to no purpose; a new
direction, if to no end; and action, if only a delaying
action before more real decisions.

All thoughts of insulation were cast aside, I was
now obsessed by the pure wild wish to get away with
her. We needed peace, away from this climate of little
quarrels. Quarrels may stimulate, but too many tend

to chip the plinth and one day the image will fall. One must be careful. Love and peace assume too often too synonymous a sound: they are more nearly opposites, and peace must be brought to love with all the care that so artificial a condition needs in a world run on conflict.

I rang her up and insisted I must see her immediately. She was settled in for one of her nights of reports and accounts. I told her to put on evening dress, I wanted to make it sound important, and so by nine o'clock we were wining and dancing, which we never did, in a restaurant with a carpet and chandeliers, with an expensive air-conditioning system blowing other people's smoke across our food, and talking about the Scillies. She looked resplendent and strange in evening dress.

'But it's *snowing*!' she said.

'Not there. And all the less in two weeks' time.'

She had to make some objection. My pop-eyed enthusiasm, high with catarrhal inebriation, must have been hard to bear. In any case, objections prove a thing, sound it out, build it.

'But what would I do on an island if they stick Bank Rate up?'

'Tell them they've found right place for it,' I wanted to say. Tell them it's the Scilly season. Tell them they're being too damned Anglo-English. But I said nothing, just watched her. I knew she was deciding. Her eyes grew distant—and then she did a most marvellous thing. As in a slow-motion film, she raised her naked right arm to pat the back of her hair, while her left hand came reaching right across her breast to extend fingertips which then slowly, slowly, like a man's hand smoothing his cheek after the razor, began to caress the soft neck-like skin of her exposed, powdered, shaved armpit. She must have been miles away—in the Scillies already. It was a magic moment.

'Agreed!' she suddenly said, and whipped her hand down.

And then: 'Oh, it'll be splendid, you know.'

'Don't let's tell anyone, not a single soul,' I said. 'Your office, yes. But otherwise let's disappear.'

She laughed and nodded, and she knew whom I meant.

I remember thinking: How could I ever have totted up so many small deficiencies against her! I had seized on a dozen molehills to make a mountain, and invented half of them at that. We rose to dance. A lot was settled, a lot put behind us. We had a good gay evening, and I loved to see her long blue eyes look so happy. When the heel of one of her shoes came off she went on dancing, gliding like a ghost, balancing on a toe, like a woman crossing a bedroom floor in her stockinged feet.

We arranged to leave London on a Sunday a fortnight ahead, and some days before this I went out at noon to buy rail tickets to Penzance at a local agency.

The thaw had set in. A few days ago icicles down the pipes had run with dark snakes of water, water had belled everywhere in the sunlit thaw, burst pipes had gushed and plumbers sprouted everywhere—the town had been soaked with water and light. Now only sun, a spring dampness, and a few gritty lumps of swept snow like huge flyblown cakes of sugar.

Among these now unbelievable snowpiles came walking towards me another wintry attempt to invalidate the sun—a girl in ski-trousers and a white sweater, with a pair of skating boots slung from laces round her neck. She looked in some way familiar. A long way off the sun glinted on the steel of the skates, which like two knives rode exactly beneath her bobbing, sweatered breasts. St. Agatha-on-Ice, I murmured, but it turned out to be Eileen, her hair dyed a pale greenish grey that framed her brightly painted face as a silver-leafed plant borders a decorative flower-bed.

'Hello! Going skating?'

'Why no,' says Eileen, 'just a light lunch with the Lord Mayor, what did you think?'

With this levity goes a bitter little leer; the whole pleasantry, if that could be the word, falls heavy as lead. One never really makes contact with Eileen: her very open-ness closes one right up.

She adds with a toss of the plant on her head: 'How's Marie?'

'Oh fine. We're going'—I nipped my tongue—'I

148

mean, she's going on very well. I didn't know you skated.'

'Marie's fault. She started Colin on it, and Colin started me. And now I can't stop, and she's too busy to come any more—too busy with you I suppose—and Colin's . . . well, he's busy too.'

'Very glad to hear he's done so well for himself.'

A kind of iridescence colours Eileen's coloured face —new life flickers behind the painted surface: 'Well, I never heard it called that.'

'But he's got this better job—the clever old so-and-so.'

'Better job? House-painting?'

'*What?*'

She grimaces: 'Well, I mean painting people's houses. With his paints I mean. Pictures, sort of.'

'But I heard from Mrs. Adrian—'

'Oh you can scrub that off, whatever he said to them. What he's doing is this scatty old idea of painting people's houses for them, as keepsakes like. But where's the people? Where's the houses? Honestly, I'm all for Colin and I wouldn't say it but to you who's one of his closest friends—'

'He said that?'

'Oh yes, he's always talking about you. But doesn't he get the soppiest . . . honest, he's more like a kid than a proper grown man I sometimes think. And what does he get out of it? Where does it get *me?* Nowhere. It gets none of us nowhere.'

'I know—but can't *you* . . .'

'I can't do anything. He's got me in wrong with my job—I don't seem to be hard at work this morning, do I? Not that I can't straighten that out with the old man—but you know what *that* means—but he's broke again, and that's another quid, which makes four in as many weeks, he thinks they grow on trees. And I bet I pay for the coffee now, he's coming out for a coffee here, I've just called on him.'

People are passing, we have to dodge to and fro to make way for them—and as her petulance rises, Eileen begins to bob up and down, while in the grey-bordered garden of her face red tides of anger battle with the rouge on her lips.

And I find myself saying: 'Can't *you* help him, Eileen? The hard way? Teach him a lesson—by saying you won't see him until he's settled . . . or something?'

Her whole face drops, and the flush of anger pales right away: 'I've tried that. It doesn't work . . .'

'Why?'

'He says okay and just stays away—and I, I can't bear it.'

Her lip is beginning to tremble, the sunlight flashes on her skates and blinds my eye. And we are still dodging to and fro and she is saying: 'I know Marie told you about that sniffing, his petrol—and me when I was in the garage. Even I thought it was a joke at first, him liking me for the smell. Not all that funny, really, either. But when I found out it was true—what do you think a girl feels then? It sounds funny I know but it's not nice—' her voice breaks, her face screws up, a big tear bulges and rolls down her cheek, Eileen's whole poor sweet armour of young contempt breaks and she stands there crying to me, helpless, hopeless, a big painted child in distress, and it is awful as she says: 'Not nice for a girl to be liked because she smells of petrol. I want to be loved for *me*.'

The sun blinds out from those skates and more tears roll down her face, diamonds in the golden sunlight. Her wet cheeks are raised to me, her nose gives a loud helpless sniff, and of all damned things, she says: 'Can't *you* help?'

There it is again!

Two, I suppose, adults face to face in the street, she crying, my eyes watering in the crisp sunlight, appealing to each other once more, all over again, to Help Colin. The tall red buses roar by, film posters shout, a high steel crane shrieks in the sky, parcel-bound women hurry, men hammer, the whole world seems on its usual feet—all except Colin closeted somewhere with a bottle of benzine and plans for a light job consonant with his dignity.

Suddenly on her words 'can't *you* help', my ears seemed to pop clear and everything became bright as thaw-water in a moment of clinical realisation—as I saw how Eileen was revealed for the first time as herself, as a pleasant grown-up child, and that it had taken Colin to do this. Never, with all her false frankness, her elaborate lack of mystery, would I otherwise have been made to feel how innocent and well-wishing she was beneath it all. Had Colin then his hidden uses? At least he had shown me I lacked the charity to have perceived Eileen clearly before this: it took him and his wake of tears to bring out feeling in me, he made me feel a dull dry clod indeed.

'Oh Christ,' she said, 'here he is,' wiping her tears, blinking, trying to make it look like the sunlight. And here indeed was Colin striding towards us smiling, brushed, clipped, in a black blazer and athletic grey trousers, fresh as a pin and plainly with not a care in the world.

Just then the doors of the cinema by which we were standing burst open and out ran what seemed a million children, a huge new milling life at thigh-level. The noise was enormous. On this amazing tide we were swept together, we could not hear whatever greetings were made, we could only mouth and sway.

The children seemed to swarm forever, more and more—but I suddenly saw that Colin might have been swaying in any case, he was not fresh as a pin at all, he had a drunken look, bright and dull at the same time.

'No, I can't come for a coffee,' I remember shouting, 'I'm late already, late for the ticket office—I mean, for something I have to do . . .'

But I was watching Colin closely. When one hears of somebody's secret vice, that person soon assumes a strange objectivity: he becomes a museum piece, and so I found myself reading Colin's face with a detached unashamed new interest, as it swung jostled by the children to and fro. I even took a furtive sniff. But he looked and smelled very much like anyone else, apart from the glassy there-but-not-there look.

Then—perhaps to cover this up I asked him whether he had been comfortable with my friends the Adrians, telling him how they had told me he had got a splendid new job.

Colin laughed: 'I'm afraid I just made that up,' he yelled. 'They're such nice people, and I don't like people worrying about me.'

I glanced at Eileen. She looked as if she had swallowed a rat.

Then as suddenly as they had arrived, the children dispersed; and, as if following suit, as if only embarrassed by the suddenly empty pavement, Eileen dragged him off to the coffee house and I turned towards the ticket agency; but now it was one o'clock, and early closing day. Too late.

The innocent impertinence of those words of Colin's was matched by a certain innocence of face—I can still see his clipped moustache, his brown eyes quickened by black lashes, his hard mobile mouth, all his frank handsome face in the sunlight declaring true sentiment and honesty. He believed, I could swear, what he said.

Colin did not calculate all the time. He did not have to. Just to present himself, penniless or in trouble, was enough to state and to win his case. I repeat: when you are in the gutter, there's always someone to pick you up—if you look clean enough. Charity is inexhaustible. You just have to move around from pitch to pitch.

But one pitch he would not have moved around from yet was Marie's. She would certainly know by now of this new development: and how would that affect her pleasure in leaving London?

I would have to act—should I get hold of him and have a real ding-dong down-to-earth talk?

'Now look here, Colin—all this has gone on long enough! You must stop stamping on other people's feet, learn to stand on your own. If you'd only be reasonable, expect a little help now and again—why, we'd all do our best for you, and willingly, but heavens man, you want to be supported *all* the time! It can't go on.'

('Oh, can't it?')

'Suppose everybody did the same? Where on earth do you think we'd be?'

(Pause. 'Everybody' never did the same. Never a good argument. Try something else . . .)

'It's all very well for you to revolt against insentient commercial hypocrisy and refuse to work in these jobs. All applause to your integrity—on paper. But you don't revolt in a vacuum. Having revolted, you accept food, shelter and money gained by other people under the same system. You're like the old lady who scolds her cat for catching a bird, and digs her teeth into a nice tasty partridge.

'Your nihilism is simply a retreat. You're a softy, Colin. Organise, fight, suffer, and die in the attempt —then your fury has some reason. As it is, it's pointless.

'I heard today that you regard me as your friend. Well, so I am. So much your friend that I'll refuse the easy way—of sentiment and charity. And choose the hard way—of checking my generosity. That's not a nice feeling for me, but it's the best way to help *you*.'

Once again I am pacing my room like a wild animal behind bars, thin-lipped and raving, and as I preach to the empty air there comes the old sneaking feeling that I choose this 'hard way' because at base I am ungenerous.

I lose my temper.

'One thing at least—keep away from Marie! If I ever hear you've seen her again, even spoken to her on the telephone—I'll smash your face in.'

As an afterthought:

'And I don't care if you do take me to court.'

But a strong hand must also be taken with Marie.

'When people fall in love, darling, they take over the loved one's friends, relatives, and this is not always pleasant. In the best of ointments there's a fly. But never a fly like Colin! Not a *bluebottle*, darling.'

(Ha ha! We are wrapping our little gun in the cottonwool of good humour.)

'Responsibilities must be shouldered. You have a crippled aunt? Very well, I'll wheel her. Your awful sister needs an audience for her dreadful bigotries? Okay, she can use my ears! But this Colin—forgetting for the moment that you've loved him, putting aside my natural jealousy of him, which you must admit is fairly trying—this Colin is not a matter of responsibility. Irresponsibility is nearer the mark. Can't you see you're presenting me with a millstone?

'You must admit—he doesn't rouse instincts of self-sacrifice. He's not like someone who has truly suffered.

'You say he has? He looks on the black side from motives of honesty? And this honesty, since it is impractible, and since he cannot *do* anything about it, transfers its impotence to his own character? So that he ends up by not being able to do anything about himself?

'Come off it, honey. *We've heard that one before.*

'Oh, he suffers from the guilt of all revolutionaries, eh? What's that—a new disease? Revolt going down in the subconscious as doing wrong, eh, even if you think it's right at the time? Acting against the common wish—naughty boy, eh? He suffers more than I know, huh?

'Baby, you have me in circles. I think I'll drop me over to the hospital and have my head out.'

Baby? Honey? A bright laconic smile spreads across my face as I sprawl in my easy chair. I'm tough as they come. Manly wise. I know all. And the little woman? Jeeze, she's just a kid anyways, and you know what you've got to do with the kiddies? Humour 'em!

And slap 'em.

I leap from my chair: 'Whether you like it or not, baby, you and I are getting on that train and clearing out of town right *now*! And baby I don't mean perhaps!'

A pause. 'I mean maybe,' I add quietly, the wind falling from my sails. 'I mean I don't mean maybe. Baby.'

On the telephone her voice had a cool, too practical ring—something was on her mind, she had plainly heard Colin's latest news. This only encouraged my new and forceful mood—but I kept quiet about it. As I ascended in the lift to see her that evening, I grew taller with enterprise, both the lift and I went up.

She swung the door open—and ran away. It was only to the interrupted telephone. I lowered my arms and walked into the flat and over to the roof-window, listening absently as she discussed a new issue of stock to be subscribed the following week. Pinkish brown clouds flew across the cold iron sky like tufts of thermogene loose in the night. And should I ever lie on that roof with her under a summer sun? Our bodies browning and the black soot gently falling, babes on the roof? Would the great gable ends rise against a hard blue sky, Italy in London, pink brick against the blue? I turned away from the window in a sudden access of apprehension—half my new aggression fell away as I saw how careful I must be to conserve us.

'The redemption yield,' said my love's voice from the bedroom, 'is reasonable, you know.'

And then:

'We'll see who's right on Wednesday, then. Fair enough?'

On Wednesday? On Wednesday we would be boating about between the islands. How could she . . . had she decided to stay? Then, looking through to the passage, I saw her travelling cases placed out against the wall—she must have got them down for a dustover. So that was all right. My spirits rose again and then she came in, brisk and smiling.

'Oh these issues,' she said. 'Darling!' And kissed me, and pushed me lightly away as I began to kiss her. Preoccupied? Very well then. The little coldness retrieved my aggression, and I plunged straight in:

'Two more days—and we'll be off.'

She made the noise of someone enjoying an appetising food smell. And then went over to the bookcase and wiped her finger along it like a bad actress in search of dust and distraction.

'I was thinking,' she said.

'. . . of spring flowers in winter, clotted cream and morning mackerel, Atlantic airs on a salt-string,' I intoned, 'but I can't *promise* the flowers . . .'

She clutched at that.

'That's exactly what I was thinking—is it, after all, the place to go? Wouldn't it be easier to go just a little way out—you know, to one of these big strange suburban hotels you talk about? The trouble is, also, there's a lot going on next week.'

'There seems to be.'

'What do you mean?'

'Oh, nothing.'

My courage collapsed. We were getting angry and short again.

'Oh, I heard you on the 'phone, this—what's it called—issue?'

'It does make it a bit difficult.'

'But, darling . . .'

For a moment she seemed less decided. 'I don't quite know what to do,' she said, speaking more to herself than to me.

'But you've got your cases out,' I said, encouragingly, pointing to the hall, 'you've already started!'

She seemed surprised, and glanced over at them sharply: 'Oh those, yes.'

'Oh come on, let it all go to the devil!' And I put my arms round her, trying to blanket her with body and words. Forceful. Characterful. Aren't men supposed to sweep women off their feet?

She pushed me away and laughed: 'I know, I know
. . . but.'

I hated that little push-away. And said sourly:

'But you've heard about Colin, is that it?'

A dreadful silence.

'What about him?' she said.

'No job again, of course.'

Casually: 'Oh that—yes.'

'And probably no roof'—and suddenly I saw what
a fool I had been and pointed at the cases. 'I suppose
they *are* yours?' I shouted.

She flared back, looking me too straight in the eyes:
'I never said they were!'

'But you let me think it, didn't you?'

She gave a little shrug to her shoulders: 'Oh well,
he had nowhere else to put them.'

She looked so much in the wrong. I wanted to help
her out of it, and somehow I felt I had to atone for it
by lying myself, it made it more equal.

'And I've bought the tickets,' I said, 'and made
reservations, and everything.'

After a moment she said: 'Can't you get them
refunded?'

I should perhaps have left it at that. Shame should
have shut me up. But I began a longer lie about paying
my account with the agency, long overdue, and that I
could scarcely take back what I had been so long paying—I stuttered all this disconsolately, adding that of
course it didn't matter.

An extraordinary thing happened. I think back on it now with disbelief—and sometimes, when I see that it did in fact happen, with less surprise than sadness.

In short, my story had its effect. The purchase of those tickets turned the tide. Colin was deserted and love was mine, so that two pieces of green cardboard might not be wasted! But why use such tragic tones? Mediocrity was the tragedy. Those two pieces of cardboard worth no more than ten pounds summed up the petty limitation of our lives, our sad restricted waste-not-want-not middle middle-class manner of living and flinching.

And I thought of Colin. Colin at least would drop two green tickets down the grating of a drain, and walk, not moved much, off down the street.

This, of course, is half his appeal. Irresponsible, he acts out what we others dream.

'What time's the train?' Marie said.

'Ten-thirty, Sunday morning.'

We speak monotonously. The station might be an execution shed. It is a lovely way to be going away.

I want to go over and take her in my arms and kiss the strain away—but I cannot risk that little push again, I am a sulker, coldness sends me sliding into my shell.

'At least,' I say in a coldly jolly voice, Colin still dropping the tickets down the drain at the back of my mind, 'you can let him have the flat while you're away.'

And she brightens.

She gives me a quick shy look of thankfulness.

However—this is so wonderful after what has happened that my heart leaps and, feeling something like love for Colin who has thus brought us together again, I suggest: 'In fact—why not go the whole hog and let him stay tonight? Only two days to go—and we've both a lot to do.'

She shakes her head, as if this were too much to believe. 'I think I will then,' she smiles.

'Do you know where to find him?'

'I expect I can.'

I had to leave then—there was a pile of work to get through. As the lift came to the ground floor, the grill revealed a flickering picture, like a badly cabled photograph, of Colin waiting: I am not sure that he had not in fact pressed the bell and pulled me down.

'Hello!' he said. 'Well met!' And he raised his eyes up the liftshaft towards her flat and gave me one of those large, conspiratorial winks.

'Hope I haven't butted in?' he said. 'She said you'd be leaving early tonight. And God knows I want a good kip. Been at it all day. *Voilà!*' He whipped out from under his arm quite a good gouache of somebody's little stucco house, a kind of Utrillo with knobs on. I said goodnight.

Then called back to him: 'I'd rather you didn't tell Marie we met. Can't explain why now. Okay?'

'Mum's the word,' he said, with another wink.

It seemed the best way to leave it. To be caught out

again would be too hard on her. 'Mum's the word' echoed in my ear: I would soon really be this man's Best Friend.

In what is called the cold light of day—and was for me the hot glare of strip-lighting in a copyist's office, and then the coffee-bar search for a substitute to play for me at Belle's, and all the rest of the luxurious low-down Tin Pan Alley life of fiddlers with frayed cuffs and electric guitarists in huge white cars, of second-hand saxophones and five-figure incomes—in this light I began by gnashing my teeth over Marie's deception but ended in absolute admiration of her. What, after all, did it add up to but that she had continued to do what she thought right in the face of every objection? She had simply stuck to her principles.

At least, I hoped there were objections. It was not for me to gauge how much she loved me—but one has to take some things for granted. I had to believe she loved me. If one retreats from this assumption, one soon leaves the picture altogether.

By the afternoon I was on the telephone to her, pouring out reassurances. She sounded relieved, and finally we talked optimistically of Colin being settled in and of us going away, a *ménage à trois* comfortably adjusted. What with so much to do, we settled not to meet again until the next evening, the Saturday before we left—when she would drop into the club for an hour or so during my last night's work.

In the meanwhile, in the confusion of extra work, a minor castigation but an awful one visited me, a rebuke straight from Above. Those green tickets had assumed so strong a reality that I forgot, until the very last moment, to buy them. Only the fact of having to race to the bank before Saturday closing time reminded me; and by the grace of a forgiving Heaven the ticket agency was late in closing and I came panting out with the sweet second-class things green and safe in my shaking guilty hand.

The same hand that lifted a glass to my lips at the bar of the New Marlven that last Saturday night when the Adrians came in, bubbling all over, pleased as the Punches they nearly resembled. But this twinkling, polished, shiny little couple seemed always lightly to bubble. Especially to notice them bubbling meant that something unusual had happened.

It had. They had been burgled.

Effusively, each delightedly telling part of the story, I heard how it had happened that afternoon, when they were out shopping, all the way over to Aldgate, they said. And somebody had got in through the front door—there were jemmy marks—and made off with all Mrs. Adrian's jewellery and Mr. Adrian's new malachite dress studs!

'But we have such lovely furs,' Otto said with wide surprised eyes, 'and they never touched them!'

This seemed to be the only matter for distress.

Otherwise, I have seldom seen a better pleased couple. Of course, it was the insurance. They didn't mind what went. They were people who liked things too much to be possessive. The more that was changed the better.

'But one thing's so funny,' Myra Adrian beamed, 'the police—of course, we had to have the police in, such nice men too—the police said the marks on the door could not have been made opening it, not that he could see. He thought they were faked. And I think he looked a bit suspicious at my Otto!' She bubbled with laughter at the idea of this. Anyone else would have been resentful—or frightened.

'Yes, an inside job they called it,' Otto said. 'And now I've got to make a list of all our daily helps—and *that's* the hell of a damn long list, the rate we change them.'

But I was already excusing myself and off to the telephone. With luck Marie had not left. And I entered upon yet another white, white lie. That I was leaving early—so much work to finish at home—and so there was no point in her coming to the club that night. And I would be round with a taxi good and early in the morning.

Our journey had taken on the urgency of an elopement.

VIII

HOUSES, factories, fields flash by as we settle down for the long day in our brown carriage smelling of stale smoke and passengers, coal-grit and fresh-printed magazines.

As a dog turns round and round before relaxing into his basket, so do we passengers fuss and test our seats, our new patch of space—adjusting our knees and feet to those opposite us, squinting for ashtrays, covertly assessing the luggage on the rack above. At first, so strong is our suspicion of the others in the carriage, we two sitting opposite each other cannot talk easily. Only a few feet apart, we look each other in the face—unusually openly, it feels—and smile. Marie makes a big sighing shrug of her shoulders to indicate that all is over, we're away.

I have a book or two on the Scillies, and hand one to her, pointing at a picture and whispering. But I raise my voice for a moment on the word 'Scillonian' to indicate to our fellow-passengers that we are bound for the very *end* of the line—we're not the kind that sneaks out at Plymouth. And that I am conversant with such a word as Scill*onian*, I talk the language.

A man on my left coughs markedly, eased by my having spoken, but having somehow to assert himself against it from behind his paper. Opposite, a woman with an involved hat crushed on her head like a little broken fruit basket spills a magazine onto Marie's lap, and on receiving it back smiles and nods effusively: 'Thanks *ever* so much!' Teeth pour out of her mouth to show what a really nice person she is.

Then from the window-seats, occupied by two scrubbed severe middle-aged women in grey coats and round grey hats, plainly nannies, a voice booms absolution on our company: 'We're clean now. It's taken us six months, but now we do our big jobs on the potty *every time!*'

This news puts the whole carriage at its ease. There are one or two furtive smiles, and a great flapping of papers, and as in a ritual dance, everybody changes legs at once.

As the train glides on through the day, we become curiously intimate with these few people known for so short a time. Yet all we learn about them will be forgotten tomorrow. One by one they clamber out to the dry land of their platforms, and one watches them disappear with luggage and packages up lanes, into cars—the lonely, the homely.

At length by a lowering evening light we leave fat Devonshire, England narrows and we enter the granite taper of Cornwall. Now one senses the presence of the sea to either side. Desolate stone stations are lined with palm-trees grey with grit. White pyramids of gleaming china-clay rise like a mirage on a moonray horizon. Magic! I nearly wake Marie to look at these.

But she is tired after the long journey. And in a way I am glad to be out of her sight for a while. It has not been too pleasant to spend the first day of our new freedom keeping the burglary under my belt, sitting there edged with deceit at a moment of greatest trust. No good telling myself that I am acting for the best: dishonesty hurts, and it seems particularly absurd to erect more defences at a moment when we should be breaking them down.

I could only try to forget all this in a quite indulgent irresponsible gladness about Marie herself, and in a number of small new graces she showed. I was watching her, I suppose, as a parent watches with unique delight his child perform some very ordinary action for the first time. We had never been in a train together before, and there—the marvel of it!—she has luggage, a new kind of townishly country coat, and a momentously assured way of crossing her nyloned legs, of smoking a cigarette, of glancing out through the window at the passing mud. Just like a small, sure, sophisticated woman travelling—but this time mine. It amazes me when, composedly, she rises and goes out into the corridor towards the lavatory. She knows where the corridor is!

But Marie is not altogether composed. Those bright dark blue eyes glitter with amusement—but nevertheless she blushes as she catches my own eyes straying to the luggage-rack and her most maidenly initials blazing out on one of the cases above her head. And when by chance my foot touches hers, and I press it, she whips her foot away as if I have stung her—no love-making, no one shall know we are illicit. Once or twice she says quite loudly such maritalisms as: 'Did we remember to stop the papers?' And unfortunately: 'Good thing we've got Colin settled in the flat—sees to the burglars at least.' I try to smile at this, and she asks me whether I feel ill.

And at times throughout the day I catch her looking at me most thoughtfully. We are both, in fact, nervously estranged by our closer companionship. So that when finally she sleeps, this little absence brings a wry relief. She looks, too, immediately innocent. No one looks more relaxed than a sleeper in a train—she is slopped to one side, one arm in the lap of her neighbour, a light snore coming through her open mouth, legs at awkwardly splayed angles. Her skin takes on a sleeper's pallor as, mysteriously, the cosmetics are consumed from within. She looks so young, and so pathetically innocent, that the shining knight inside me—or is it the district nurse?—wants to take her in my arms and sing a protective lullaby.

The night must be spent at Penzance, and we have a lovely nervous time entering the hotel. I am quite as uneasy as she is, and as over-sure of myself. Together we put on a confounding playlet for the porter and the reception clerk. It is made plain that we are in no hurry to get into that bedroom together. 'I'll go on up, dear

—you go and have a drink,' she says airily, who has never called me 'dear' before.

And I am left illegibly writing my name in the register. Later I sip a whisky in the bar feeling as if there was left somewhere behind me a chintzy little house and a runabout and two thumping great kids thankfully at school—Daddy needs a rest, and Mums too, come to that. But it is good to reflect that she has overacted her part, showing she is not at all used to it; and to consider that, had this been a casual affair, we would have taken a very opposite attitude, probably brazening out our metropolitan naughtiness in the face of what we might have ungenerously dubbed as bourgeois, sheep-faced provincials.

By the middle of the next day we have said 'dear' to each other so often that it has ceased to be artificial. A fine inter-possessive ease has overtaken our relapsed nerves. And when finally the *Scillonian* comes nosing round the rocks of St. Mary's, an unembarrassed and delighted young married couple stand at the rail.

Thus we had at least some few dozen hours of married bliss before the letter came.

Even my guilty secret worked finally to our profit: it made an added risk, it make me feel relentless, ruthless, burning my boats and throwing them to the winds.

The hotel, with its planked bar-room and photographs of wrecked three-masters, its white and black figurehead among veronica in a green Atlantic garden, its gull-cries down the chimney and its few flighty modern furnishings, gave us our first feelings of permanence together. Discovering which side she liked to sleep on. Watching her take possession of drawers. Idling by the window, simply to hear her moving about behind me. Savouring the lack of urgency, lulled by the fiddle-fiddle-fiddle of womankind filing nails, doing and re-doing hair, face-painting, dress-hitching, forever changing cardigans and scarves against the changing temperature: sounds of nurse or mother pottering through the echoes of a childhood afternoon.

We have travelled from winter into spring. There is strength in the sun's warmth: sheltered from the sea-breeze behind a wall, with a camelia tree flowering rose against a deep blue sky, one could imagine oneself in a draughty corner of the true South. Away from the cream-tea whirl of Hughtown, the islands are beautifully deserted—yet inhabited enough to avoid desolation. Paths rather then roads, and, among high green hedges, the surreal glimpse of farmers in navy blue, gumbooted and peak-capped, delicately tending their dancing fields of daffodils.

And the coastguard standing against his white house in a tall round sailor's hat, a Russian priest against his Crimean chapel. Big fat black sows lying about like lumps of basalt—and like the black lumps of rounded rock discovered at low tide among carpets of yellow sand skirled with sepia seaweed and beaded with shallow turquoise pools. Breezes blow, bringing a strangely sighing music of sea, a song that is supposed to have sent men mad on the marooned outer rocks. But to us so much wide wild air only deepens the ancient mystery of stones and barrows and untrod salt turf.

We boated to Bryher, hilly and wild, and Marie who still wore the highish heels of some kind of weather-proof boots on her sparrow feet, looked tartly out of place, as if she had been dropped from an airliner. City-bred man should always take his girl to the country: there she looks properly isolated, fresh and vulnerable, a good test for the main barometer of love, his protec-tive instinct. Marie looked doubly vulnerable in her London clothes, and her slight orientalism quickened against the austere Celtic stones. My own mercury showed high pressures.

Like the stones, our bed and its room seemed to receive us as its only guests. A stray hairpin in a drawer, a used razor blade on a widowsill announced no recent visitor but someone now dead who had stayed there many, many years before. We claimed the place as our own.

Into this room, on our second day, the chamber-maid brought a letter.

It was from Otto Adrian. Having had to call in the police, on account of the insurance company, he had to be of what help he could to them—and they wanted Colin's address. Only a formality, of course. Everyone who had been in the flat had to be interviewed. They wouldn't trouble Colin. They had a clue, Otto cheerfully added, the mark of a rubber-soled shoe—of all things stating its brand-name, Ducksweather, and Otto's pen laughed at having Ducksweather written all over the flat. But Colin would soon show he hadn't any shoes of this kind. Otto apologized for troubling me.

He must have got the address from Belle. I had left Belle my address for some reasonless umbilical reason—who finally goes absolutely free?

We were lying on the bed. I had not risen when the chambermaid came in, since we were reading and the bed was covered with books and papers and I was proud of this settled, marital look of things. But now with the letter in my hand, and Marie beside me— what could be done? To tell a lie at a distance, well-prepared, is one thing: to act one, on the spur of the moment, slap in the face of one's friendly love, is quite another. It was too underhand. And too dangerous.

Halfheartedly I lowered the letter, as if bored with it. Without looking at her, I waited. Either we were so intimate that we respected each other's private affairs; or our intimacy was so unfamiliar and precious that it would feel cold not to ask to share such an event as a letter. I knew Marie would be thinking all this too—and when she was warm enough to put out her hand for the letter, a puff of love went out to her before my heart sank right down.

'Oh, the Adrians had some little burglary,' I said casually. 'I suppose the police have to see everyone ...'

But she was reading quickly.

'God,' she said. 'Oh God.'

Then we lay there silent, propped up side by side. I remember not knowing where to look, staring absurdly straight ahead at the foot of the bed.

She spoke slowly and quietly: 'I know why you didn't tell me, of course,' she said, 'and I suppose I should thank you.'

There was nothing to say.

'But I *won't*,' she said, raising her voice, 'it's never any good running away from these things. You're a fool!'

Nothing to say.

'What was stolen?'

'A little jewellery ... but look, we don't know it's him.'

'Of course it is! He got a key cut. Anyhow'—and she quietened and looked guilty—'I gave him those shoes.'

That was the worst news yet. Superstitions were inevitable. Now she would feel herself to blame.

'Naturally, I shan't answer this letter,' I said.

'I don't know what to do,' she said.

'You won't write either,' I said.

'Oh?'

But she was too concerned to take offence. 'I ought to warn him', she said, 'but what good'll that do?

They'll always be after him now—oh, the bloody
fool! But at least he'd better lose those shoes!'

The vision instantly rose of her in a cell, accessary
after the fact.

'For God's sake don't *write* that,' I said quickly.
'Don't sign it. Don't do it.'

'Of course I must.'

Then I went for her.

I went for her systematically, using every argument
I could, speaking hard and cold, warm and loving by
turns. I put the whole question of myself-and-her-and-
Colin. I went on and on and on. I would never have
risked it in London. But we were on an island. There
would always be time to get her back before she got
away.

She tried to interrupt. I overspoke her. I saw her
simply sitting round-eyed and numb, following my
mouth like a fascinated rabbit-mouse. I suppose, I am
sure that what I said of our love, or of my love for her,
moved her. But what finally persuaded her was something quite different. For unconsciously I was talking
like a woman, not like a man with his pauses and
struggle for logic, his indirections; but like a woman
pouring it all out unashamed, repeating myself,
pouncing from one thought to the other, direct and
honest and absolutely unfair: I was out for what I
wanted and got it.

She put her head on my shoulder, and cried,
quietly, like a child too tired to cry, snivelling. And

this, and in any case, the sense of success, made me feel brutal, and I myself suggested she should telegraph, though *not* to give our address.

But I was not the only woman about. Later, she telephoned him.

I saw her off to the telegraph office and walked out onto the harbour wall. The Atlantic sunset did its best to help my foreboding. A low red sun was made huge by a pearled sea-mist, and the islands floated out to sea like the very end of all lost land and time, disappearing over the edge of a wet world like every other golden moment never to be regained. And I thought how this holiday was now overshadowed and might end in similar darkness. Then my eye caught a sudden flash of flame in the hold of a moored trawler. Furnaces? No. Crates of yellow daffodils flaring false yellow flame in the sunlight, cold as yellow can be. However —a sign of hope? Or of false hope?

I stood there attracting symbols to myself, they stuck to me like burrs. At dinner that night Marie was preoccupied, trying to be bright, but well away with her worrying again. Ordinarily we would have marvelled at the new things about—for instance the up-to-date uninsular talk of the islanders in the bar, world affairs discussed with a grasp clear and far less parochial than a Londoner's. And we would have remembered the bright tractors, scarlet and pale blue, sawing like giant beetles over the green island hills.

And so on . . . but we did not. We talked like strangers about the food and things more immediate. Once I tried an old game on her. It does not, on the surface, sound a kind game—but its reason was purely a delight in watching her face move. It was to ask her a simple and intimate question about herself—such as 'Do you consider yourself goodlooking, pretty, beautiful?'—and watch the result pour out.

That night it did not work at all. 'That's a rather leading question,' she smiled. And that was all.

But she tried to be companionable, she dragged up this or that topic by the grit of her teeth—we would have done better to sit silent. Yet she did try, and that was nice of her. Once more I had to tell myself—she's not to blame. You can't blame someone for feeling charitable. Just my bad luck, just bad luck.

We did not speak much about Colin. There was little to say. He had plainly committed theft, the matter had got into the hands of the police and there was no turning back from that.

'I suppose any Ducksweather Treadware marks might have been left over from when he stayed in the flat,' I said once.

She was about to answer but stopped herself, simply shook her head.

We went to bed early. She took up a book. She read until after twelve. Sometimes I caught her eyes looking above the page, thinking—but still pretending to read. I put down my own book earlier; and waited.

It was only our third night together: but I knew she was reading herself to sleep, and we lay there nervously constrained with each other, running a kind of race, waiting each other out.

Then, after a long time, the artifice of such a strain —which drummed up into a quiet kind of enmity— suddenly seemed so stupid, two lovers lying alone in bed tucked up in an inn on an island with miles of protective sea around, two breathers breathing, nearly touching but each enormously alone—and I reached out my arm and put it round her shoulders, drawing her towards me. We can lose ourselves, I thought, ride over this wall and lose ourselves in what lies waiting on the other side.

The instant I touched her she said clearly, as if the words had been waiting on her lips: 'Darling, have you opened the window?'

In the first place, a command to do something else, a delaying device. And in the second, the open window meant cold night air, the end of intimacy, the last act before sleep.

I just said: 'No.' And snatched my hand away. Very bad things overcome me at the suspicion of coldness. I am quick to take offence. I sulk. I grow steel-cold myself. Little boy left out, I swear to see anyone in hell before I'll make another move.

The instant I took my hand away the question came, with wide wise eyes: 'Why do you take your hand away?' Making me instantly feel foolish. Putting the blame on me. An old trick, and the most damnable of the lot.

I threw myself on her, gritted down my sulking in a biting black shut-eyed kiss, and her arms came round me, her body moved. We began to make love—but there was less love than determined lust. Whatever a cold woman does, however much she acts, there is a presence lacking and a man is seldom fooled. I opened my eyes and saw hers staring up past my shoulder at the ceiling. Gently I turned away onto the bed by her side. 'It's no good,' I said, 'is it?'

She was nearly crying: 'Oh, my darling—I'm so sorry.' She shook her head and looked away. 'I'm so upset,' she said.

We lay for a few minutes in silence. I took her hand in mine. But even her hand was not truly there. Then I went to the window and opened it, turned out the light, and lay beside her empty and hopeless, nothing to say and no sleep. Boots passed clattering on the paving beneath the window, loud and very near, as if they too were in the room with us.

Wide awake, with the darkness sparkling alive. I could hear her breathing, irregularly, sometimes more a sigh than a breath: and then a greyness of light began to frame the frilled curtains past the foot of the bed—the moon, or a harbour light somewhere along the quay?—and lying in the dark bed this light was the only thing to look at, it was as attractive as a night-light to a child, and the eyes raced in the dark to see if it lit up anything else in the room, a dark hanging coat, the gleam of a dead mirror.

Once she moved restlessly beside me; then lay still: and I felt she was holding herself still, pretending sleep. I remembered how once in the country I had heard a church clock strike one—and how lonely in the grave cold night that single stroke had sounded. Could one have heard it? A single bell needs another to confirm it. I lay there waiting for a similar bell, suddenly terrified that I would miss it even if it struck —and as my ears were straining in the dark for a distant sound all the bed clothes seemed to rise nearby, so much sound so near, and she was up and had the light on.

'Darling, I've done a dreadful thing. I don't know how to say it.'

Her hair was dishevelled, a wetness of cream glistened on her face. In her white nightdress, and thus suddenly in the night, she looked like a woman who has seen a ghost and like a ghost herself at the same time. She began to walk about the bedroom, and I thought of her bare feet getting cold. 'When I telephoned Colin today—'

'*Telephoned!*' I said.

'But you know I telephoned,' she said.

'We said telegraph.'

'Oh, then, I must have thought—' and a slight sly smile.

'But we wrote the telegram down.'

She let her arms fall slackly, shoulders bowed, and I felt like a bully.

'Never mind,' I said, 'what is it?'

'I didn't want to tell you, I thought at least we'd have tonight together—but as it is . . .'

'What do you mean—tonight?'

She looked frightened. One of her shoulder straps had fallen, showing her naked breast. What might have looked erotic looked only terribly defenceless, flesh robbed of spirit, sadly ordinary. She bit her lip, then forced it out:

'He's coming down tomorrow.'

I suppose, looking back, I might have known. But then, I had built up such hope. Now I was too shocked for anger. One hears of the death of a friend, and the first question is 'How?'—before there is time to be moved.

'Why?' I said.

'He's got to get away.'

'But why *here*, why when this is our holiday, our time together . . .'

She sat down on the bed and stared at the wall opposite: 'He's got nowhere else.'

Now the anger came. 'Why always *you*?' I shouted. 'He knows a hundred other people. Besides, it's damned silly asking him here. It's the most dangerous kind of place you could choose.'

Her face fell. She looked like a child not knowing.

'It's an island?' she asked.

'And with very few people on it, and the best place to be noticed, and miles of sea around. You might as well have put him in jail. The only place he could disappear in is a town, a big town.'

'I thought—these French trawlers in the harbour —they go across to Brittany.'

'Oh, Marie . . . this isn't a film.'

'It's not over heroic to bribe someone, is it? We've got the money with us.'

'And what does he do in Brittany for the rest of his life? What does he eat? Onions?'

She flared up: 'Don't be funny.'

Then as quickly burst into sobs: 'It's not only that, it's worse. You don't know what he's like, he's talked of killing himself before, twice, and now he's started this petrol again, that's dangerous enough, but it puts his judgement all out, he's not balanced.'

'But he *hasn't* killed himself, has he?' I said coldly. 'It's talk, everyone knows that kind of talk.'

'But one doesn't *know*,' she sobbed. 'Don't you see one doesn't *know*.'

'Oh come on, the common reason for suicide is revenge. That's why so many people half-do it. And that's why there's so much talk about it in any case.'

'I don't believe it! I think that every time he talks he gets nearer to it. Like with other things—when you talk about them, things become possible. You wait till someone you love talks about it, you wait, you just don't *know*!' she cried.

The word 'love' fell like a cold stone in my stomach. 'All right,' I said. 'Then he's coming tomorrow.'

I felt abruptly tired of it all. 'All the same, you're doing him a bad turn getting him here.'

She only repeated: 'But I must help him.'

'The only intelligent way to do that is to prescribe what really will help him. As it is, you're only helping yourself.'

'Oh Christ, isn't it natural to help someone when they're ill? When you pick a man off the pavement, you don't expect to cure him?'

'You'd cook a goose for a man with a liver attack,' I said, and to end it turned out the light.

I lay there hating her, Colin, everything. 'Pray God they put the sod in gaol,' I thought, 'quick.' And then I thought of our beautiful love affair, and this fine new bucket of water thrown over it. 'I'll get the cold cream treatment tomorrow night, the dear old cold night-cream slapped on before she goes to bed,' I thought, 'and the day after it'll be the curse.'

But she lay there shaking with sobs in the dark, making no noise, and I felt the terribly slow big tears welling from her eyes and in a minute all the hate had gone and she was in my arms now loudly sobbing and I was comforting and stroking and loving this poor beloved thing whom above all, and far oh far above taking pleasure from, I wanted to save and protect.

The next day dawned deep with fog. We sat in bed

with our breakfast tray listening to the long moaning sounds of a signal somewhere out to sea, staring at the blank grey windowspace, trying to be normal.

Once again I had to repeat to myself: This is life. Everyone has a skeleton hanging about the cupboards of his life, usually another person, and this happens to be mine. It is nothing extraordinary. Face up to it.

And another voice said: But isn't the clanking of these bones too loud? To be followed out into the Atlantic during the most blessed days of the year, perhaps of a lifetime—to have to hand over all our means of being there to the skeleton and a Breton trawlerman, and ourselves to take the train, tails between legs, back to London? Isn't there a way out? And I daydreamed about being rich—I would buy Colin a chicken farm, I'd send him to the other end of the world, buy him a gold mine . . . but even as I dreamed of it, I knew he'd be back, something would go wrong, the rot was deep inside him and the rot was dependence—whatever it was, mother-wish, wish for womb, wish to impress, whatever the dear old useless-to-know motive, it was there, and I couldn't see any reason for it not to go on erupting for ever. Gold mines are nothing to this kind of property.

Would the fog stop the *Scillonian* coming in? A foolish hope—as one might hope to delay any inevitable happening for a few hours, and only for those few hours—took me to the window.

A wet warm fog. One could imagine it wreathing

with a falsely tropical flavour round the tall palms on
Tresco, it was like a warm soaked grey sail, muffling
everything—muffling those other palms in the granite
churchyard, and the gravestones that gave so many
names of the drowned and of those who had died
aboard ship of cholera and yellow fever. This strange
fog matched the graves, the palms, all this Celtic
Capricorn: but now the sun was beginning to shine
through like a round pearl collar stud. It was lifting.
The *Scillonian*, booming its way over dead calm water,
would be nosing in after noon.

But there was no need to have bothered about the
boat, the ordinary inexpensive boat—Colin arrived
by air towards midday.

He came into the hotel long before we were ready
for him. He was wearing an old military-looking rain-
coat, with epaulette-flaps on the shoulders, and he
looked tired but determined. All he seemed to be
worried about was the aeroplane: 'Landed on this
fearfully tilted field,' he said, slanting his hand. 'Nearly
threw the whole inner man up. Talking of which,' he
said, 'a drop of something wouldn't hurt. I suppose
they're open? Should we adjourn?'

He had been drinking already—or possibly sniffing
—and seemed worried about getting a drink quickly.
He said nothing about arriving so suddenly or why—
but perhaps he thought the gentlemanly thing was to
maintain some reserve on this. Marie, however, was

staring at his feet: 'Good God, you've got them on!' she said.

He looked down and laughed: 'Oh, the old Duckswear? You don't expect they're going to'—and he dropped his voice to a stage whisper—'follow me *here* with their magnifying glasses?'

Plainly he was out to make light of the whole affair. This, of course, was truly infuriating—but I held my tongue. Marie would have turned on me. I, who had every reason for anger, had to keep quiet; she, the willing Samaritan, was the one who could give him hell. So it goes. And so she did. She called him a fool in different ways for five minutes, five long minutes and two large whiskies, among the wrecks in the bar. He let himself be lashed: sometimes he looked down at his glass, sometimes he stared at her in a lost, surprised way. But he was pretending, he was really enjoying this attention—it never mattered what form it took, it was attention. And somewhere behind that stiff-upper-lipped face, with its clipped moustache and plastered hair, and the military straight neck that propped it up, there was a leathery old twinkle. I suppose Marie saw it too, for she finally tailed off: 'But *why* did you do it? You weren't broke . . .'

The twinkle came into the open. He gave a wise shake to the head: 'Who's said who's done what?'

'Oh, Colin!'

'I'm not saying nothing,' he said, laughing.

Marie turned away, and swore under her breath: 'After they'd been so bloody good to you.'

It must have been her turning away, the end of attention, that washed off his laugh. He said, suddenly bitter: 'They're pretty well fixed up, I should say. That nicely lined little nest wouldn't miss a few odds and sods. But tell us,' he said brightly, 'what goes on here? What's it like?'

She turned on him: 'Dangerous,' she said, 'and for God's sake throw those damned shoes away.'

He tried again to laugh it off: 'An island? And, I believe, one policeman? Don't expect he's got as much as a notebook.'

But Marie interrupted him and explained about the French trawler. He listened attentively now. But when she finished, said slowly: 'It's very kind of you both —but honestly, what on earth would I do in France? No, my love, it's very dramatic but I can only see a long flat French road and an empty tummy. Now if only I was our friend here'—and he clinked his glass at mine—'I could play them their pianos.'

'It wouldn't be easy,' she said. 'But at least it isn't a dead end, like here. You've got to do something.'

He shrugged his shoulders and said, quite sincerely and gravely: 'Why must one always *do* something? Why does one always think something *can* be done? Aren't there some things nothing can be done about? Why don't we face that?' he said.

'Because we're human,' I ponderously began,

'and we only live in hope and our faith in what we can—'

'You know where you can stick your faith and hope—'

'Charity too?'

His duck's back let it go like water, he stamped his Ducksweather shoes on the floor and said: 'No trawler. Trawler's out.'

'Then you'll have to live on the run,' I said.

He laughed again: 'What's the odds? I do that in any case.'

Marie looked helpless and ugly. When she had sworn at him she had lost all the poise of her features, her face had opened and sagged in a beaten way near to tears and she had looked slatternly: that is something else he was able to do for her.

It was hard to hold on to my patience. I suggested that we went out and walked on the quay—at least to look at the trawler. It was something to do. There was no point in hanging about the bar all day. Marie shrugged indifference. Colin was delighted. If anything, he seemed in a holiday mood. And he was drinking enough to keep it so.

It was probably mostly to keep him away from the bar that Marie agreed when he suggested we take a boat over to Tresco or somewhere. It was the routine of the islands—and there seemed no point in not following it. We had some sandwiches made up, fixed him with a room, and were lucky enough to find a boat almost immediately—for this was not always too easy, even at a price, among a busy, leisurely people.

And so, as we chugged away from the granite quay past the French trawler, making a sound to town-heavy ears less like a motor-boat than a petrol-popping concrete-mixer, so we three estranged together in the same boat began in earnest a most unusual day.

Once on the water, Colin reached into his trench-coat pocket and pulled out a flat full bottle of whisky. He laughed when he saw Marie wince, and patted the other pocket: 'More where that came from,' he said, '*not* to worry. Nothing like a bender to straighten you up.'

So he was off on a 'bender'. The boatman smiled convivially, took a sip, and droned out his jovial tripper-talk about the passing points of interest. But otherwise Colin was by himself in this, alone in the same boat, sucking at the bottle like a big weathered baby. We listened dully to the boatman. There was nothing to do but let time pass—and of course, as usual, let the problem of Colin go free-wheeling round the mind. But one could not put it into words any more: even the gramophone with the broken record eventually runs down.

The low Spring tide exposed wide new stretches of weeded rocks and sandy islets that sent the sea-birds screaming mad. Once, the boatman pointed to what looked like a round-topped grey-specked milestone sticking from the water. I remembered the Lyonesse stories, and how traces of man-made field walls had been found under-water hereabouts. But a milestone seemed exaggerated. However, it was a seal.

One does not see a seal's head popped up from the sea everyday; but I found myself looking at it with little interest—once again the old boredom had come slopping in, like a dream of the other life before I had met Marie.

I looked over at Colin and tried to feel savage. No good. The dullness had taken over like a protective blanket, which it might well have been. Glum thoughts revolved. Accidie the antidote—the only true escape from the daily round: drink, travel, hobbies are minor escapes compared with truly elevated boredom. It lowers you above *everything*. Here we have a true state of pure waiting, properly in communion with death, all life a death-wait on the start-finish *prinzip*. Like smoking a cigarette, completing a meal, going to sleep, we always want to finish things off, ourselves too . . . I looked over at Colin almost with admiration, he really got inside one, right under your skin—and then I thought of the dreadful liquids that flow about us inside from one wettish bag of revolting gristle to another, the innards we all wear under our innocent-looking skins. 'Boy, there's things inside you you wouldn't like to see on a plate.'

I reached to Colin for the whisky bottle and took a good swig. It did no good. I was far too flat for liquor.

But half an hour later I asked for the bottle again, for the opposite reason, for liquor's best reason—to increase pleasure already perceived. For now we were standing in the amazing tropical gardens of Tresco, tall palms towering above grotesque figure-heads torn from long-foundered ships, white-eyed mermaids peering from the yucca, flowers and sun and striped shade—yet with a clean northern wind blowing fresh salt through these wonderfully misplaced luxuri-ances. Paradox and beauty, boredom's two great enemies, overcame everything else; and grasping at a sudden bright elation I took a deep drink to taste this scene fully and fix it forever.

I remember, as whisky and beauty together caught at my throat, gazing amazed at a giant blue echium, a kind of flame-blue poker starting up bee-hungry from its quiet green nest of leaves: and as the mind opened to this, so it opened wide to receive everything else—including one absurdly obvious idea which none of us had yet thought of. A wonderful idea, and absolutely watertight. It included my own salvation, and it was this: The only way the police would ever find Colin was through Marie; if Marie were separated from him, for good, he had a reasonable chance of going quite free.

One could dismiss the possibility of the Adrians spotting him somewhere: they did not want their old jewellery back, and besides they were too kindhearted. Dismiss that, and what other connection was there but Marie? And if she did not know where he was . . . ?

The Adrians had got my address from Belle. Obviously the police would have found out from the club that Colin was a friend of a woman friend of mine, and connect him with that woman. Belle knew now where Marie lived. For all we could tell, the porter might already have let them in to Marie's flat, perhaps he was doing so at this moment; and all over the floor would be Ducksweather marks and whiskers in the basin or whatever they look for . . . and I had a vision of the afternoon 'plane coming across the sky from Cornwall, an angry dot with a sting in it, cold blue plainclothed eyes and a snap of handcuffs and all the rest.

It was immediately obvious that Colin must be got off the island as quickly as possible. And that there-after he and Marie should never meet. It was the only way—and what a wonderful one.

We had all drifted in separate directions. I could see Marie at the end of the long path standing under a group of tree-ferns like a fashion model in her formally cut tweeds. Colin sat on a nearby seat in contented alcoholic silence, fuchsia drooping its red and purple bells all round him.

Now that he had to go I warmed to him again, poor fellow. The three of us! We are apt to accept patterns, as long as they are not physically repellent, simply as patterns; and Colin had become in a way a habit, if a bad one.

When in a few minutes I explained myself, and the urgency, they both had to agree, it made such absolute common sense. But Colin was the only one of us who seemed to feel no mood of disaster when we found the boatman had crossed over to the opposite island for an hour. That cancelled any chance of catching the afternoon plane back to Cornwall.

All we could do was walk about the island while we waited—and walk we did, as being the best way to keep him exercised against the whisky and in any case to offset our own impatience. One could not just sit about. Over we went to white and lonely sands on the other side of the island, a Pacific view, and to the churchyard with its dwarf palms gleaming a northern madness of yellow lichen.

We stood about in silence. Pecked at a sandwich. Walked back. Time ticked up loud against so timeless an atmosphere. I tried once or twice to talk to Marie, but she stayed very quiet. I wondered what she was thinking. I am not sure, even with so much happening, that it was not mostly disapproval of the whisky, the silent shell of a woman faced with a man and his bottle.

At last the blue-jerseyed boatman came strolling up the quay. Colin got into the boat without lurching. Then the boatman, who chugged us comfortably on the calm low-tide water over to another island— 'Agnes and Gew', he called it—told us he would be a couple of hours or more on various errands among the people on the island. 'Can't let the Turks down,' he said jovially.

N   193

'The who?'

'The Turks. Agnes folk're always called Turks. Don't ask me why. Always has been.'

'You seem to have come home,' I said to Marie, but none of us smiled, and Colin did not even hear. I suppose we could have persuaded the man to take us back there and then—but in fact there was no vital reason to offer, even to ourselves. The 'plane had been missed, we were seabound and that was that, so politely we watched him walk away from the miniature jetty up a miniature hill to where roofs showed.

Now no palms but the barren beach of a narrow cove, and higher up only windswept gorsey earth: this was an outer island fringing the Atlantic itself, weathered and wild.

We had got tired of walking and settled down by the beach to take a sunbath, probably to doze off. The sun was still warm, shining at a low angle that threw each boulder and pebble into bright light and shade, sparkling the place clear and clean and lively. Marie, still silent, as if she were finished with the whole affair, made a cushion of my coat and stretched herself out on the turf. A few yards off a solitary gull, sitting on her eggs, glanced at us sideways from currant eyes, then painfully closed them.

Colin and I walked a few hundred feet away to where the beach ended in a rise of sand across which we could see the Atlantic horizon. I suppose this odd sight of more sea over the end of a cove was what took us there. It turned out to be a bar of sand only a few yards across forming a low-tide bridge between St. Agnes and a smaller island over the way. Thus our cove was really a channel interrupted only by this curious bar. I had a map on me, and the other island was marked as Gugh—'Gew', as the boatman had said it. The sand-bar had a cart-track and footsteps on it.

'Shall we sit here and look at Gugh,' Colin said, 'or shall I go over there and look at yugh?'

'The less Duckswear on that sand the better,' I said, looking at the cart-track. 'Let's stay here.'

'I wouldn't mind a bathe,' he said.

'On top of all that whisky? You'd be mad. Besides, the water's damn cold this time of year.'

'Still,' he said looking at the calm water in our pool of a cove, clear and low like pond-water. The sea was the other side, a different matter. The sea looked deep across the bar, and piled up onto a high level, as if the bar was a dam. 'Still,' he said, 'it looks good. And I've a most respectable pair of pants on.'

He took a big swig at the whisky and flung off his coat. I was surprised to see how thin his arms were. His shirt-sleeves were already rolled up—frayed cuffs?—and the arms were starved white and the more brittle and papery for long black hairs striping them. It came as a shock. He looked as if he really had lacked food, which one never quite believed.

I told him again: 'Don't go in, you've had too much to drink. You'll get cramp, or whatever it is.'

He turned on me, abruptly vicious: 'Oh, balls to your no,' he snapped. 'Aren't you satisfied yet? You pulled a nice fast one this afternoon, didn't you?'

'I did?'

'Getting me off the island and away from Marie for good. Very convenient.'

'It was just common sense.'

The moustache scrub twitched into a half-smile. His eyes again twinkled that hard amusement, appraising, looking right into me—I had the sudden impression of the bullying small power of a prep-school master. And that was indeed what he often looked like with the firm-jawed Flandery cut of his face. Such faces must often have been masters to my generation.

'Common sense?' he said. 'And how about the common sense of the trawler idea? You didn't take to that with quite the same delight, did you? However —who's as pleased as bloody Punch now?'

'You've drunk too much,' I said.

But he had hit on an uncomfortable truth—he had made himself innocent and me guilty, so that once again he had me stuttering to excuse myself: 'Anyhow —the trawler wasn't really common sense was it?'

He increased his contempt by not answering. 'Do what you damn well like,' I said. 'Drown yourself!'

And I turned away to walk back to where Marie was lying.

But he was after me, tucking his hand round my arm: 'No offence, old thing,' he laughed, breathing whisky round into my face, 'I know I've butted in.

'I know how you feel about her,' he said.

And that was about the worst thing he could ever have said. I could only take it one way by now. I stopped and disengaged my arm. I looked him carefully in the eye and said: 'I often wonder whether you do.'

He knew what I meant. His eyes gave a little leap of life.

At that moment, very much alone on that ancient turf, with the wide sea-wind isolating us, two men alone together with stones and earth and sea and sky, primitive, a climate for declaration—he could have killed my heart with a few words, if necessary making them up. But he did not.

'Oh,' he laughed, 'nothing like that between us, if you mean her and me. Nothing like that, old boy.'

I looked harder at him and saw he meant it.

I suppose Colin was hardly ever interested in gratuitous harm. Or perhaps the whisky was at work? A second later he made a big circle with the bottle, describing the sky and the islands: 'Oh what a wonderful world,' he sang—but I saw a sadness in his eyes. 'Prison,' I thought. 'Damn, he's thinking of prison.'

His eyes followed the windswept sideways flight of a gull immensely free against the blue—and then lost with the bird's flight I saw his free hand creep up from his pocket and flash something small and silver near his nose. He seemed to take a deeper breath of the wide salt air.

It was a miniature flask. He caught me looking and tried to hide it with the palm of his hand, then lowered it to his pocket and looked away. It was the first time I had ever seen a look of guilt on his face.

'I'm going off out of the wind to have a snooze,' I said, partly to help him. 'Over where Marie is.'

'Me for the briny, then!' he brightly said.

To exaggerate his great good health? To leave us alone? Anyway, I was thankful—for one odd effect of his presence that whole day had been to keep me, willingly, away from Marie. I did not want to appear possessive: it would have felt unfair.

We walked back and he went down towards the water, which was also sheltered from the wind, while I climbed up to sprawl down a few yards away from Marie.

I saw him feel the water with his hand, and then go back and sit near, watching it. Marie was fast asleep. After our bad night and the exhausted nerves of the day she must have let herself easily and blankly go off —and since the boatman would only be back in his own time, it did seem the best thing to do. So I too lay back and tried to doze away.

The sea-wind over on the bar had drummed my ears deaf: now in this comparative shelter they relaxed open, with the pleasant feeling of ears popping clear after height. And as I began to doze it seemed a good world, everything around was so wide and free, reducing to nothing the tangled quarrel of three minute human figures sprawled on so small a patch of the whole immense mineral globe.

Sunlight caught the roof of a house on Gugh: for a moment it looked grouted with white cement, like one or two of the other cottages, and thinking of cement, I saw in my closing mind's eye the bright giraffe-like pattern of walls made of mortared granite lumps, and then glanced lazily back at Marie with the white Spring sun on her pale stockings and a tweed coat that itself looked mortared with a check pattern, and dozed further off . . . and once I thought I heard a 'plane coming in, droning through the dozing, an ominous thunder of distant violins, and dreamily imagined the black speck traversing the blue and welcomed it as much as feared it . . . wanting disaster I did not want, dozing off in a dichotomy for two, me and my other self, free-willed and determined, alone and with the herd, predatory and humble . . . while the plane-buzz may not have been more than the first and last heard tremble of a snore in my own nose.

Marie had all my clothes off. She was ripping the labels out and stitching in labels with Colin's name on them, torn from Colin's clothes. Colin was filling my pockets with his own effects, wallet and handkerchief and letters. He had shaved his moustache—how, on this wild island?—and wore black glasses. He looked ten years younger, and full of energy. They worked quickly, yet with absolute assurance, and kept smiling at each other in conspiracy—and I tried to move but a weight held my chest, they were plainly going to leave me on the island as Colin . . . and I forced up against the weight and awoke abruptly to see the landscape quite changed and dull with doom, like a country seen through tinted glass.

I looked round anxiously—but Marie was still asleep on the turf some yards to my right. I felt my own sleep had lasted a minute only. Yet it must have been longer—the world had changed, the sun had travelled round and downwards, the light no longer shone on the beach opposite and the colours of the sea and the land had dulled.

It was like coming out from an afternoon cinema into daylight, but into a different daylight, when you know you have missed so much of the day and feel uneasy and alerted to this, guilty of squandering so much time in the dark.

I rubbed my eyes—the bad dream still held me with its doomed reality—and looked for Colin. He was down lying in the edge of the water, body in, head on the sand. He was naked but for his underpants. He looked terribly thin and white.

The whisky bottle was still gripped in one of his hands which lay within the shallow edge of water, and as I blinked and shook my head to believe—for it was much colder now, and it looked mad for him to lie

naked in the water at that time of day and of year—
as I blinked I seemed to see double, for another whisky
bottle went floating, bobbing past him, gathering
speed as it went, and then my eyes opened coldly clean
to realize he had drunk both bottles, he was not asleep
but unconscious drunk, and the tide had risen steeply
and was rising still.

It was pouring in from the deep sea over the bar,
now underwater. The confluence of two rising tides
coming from different directions had formed a chopped
fast-swirling race, I saw the bottle spin away—and
then Colin's feet moved. The water was dragging at
him. I opened my mouth to shout—and then slowly
closed it. I lay without moving, even half-closed my
eyes as if I were asleep, and watched.

The water came on and lifted his legs higher. They
swung together to one side, as if he were doing an
exercise from the waist. He must have been very drunk
—doesn't a simple bucket of cold water wake a drunk?
And yet this was coldly creeping water, cold as a
wetted bed, chilling right into the bone. Perhaps he
was already dead . . . and I wondered whether I was
really awake, yet knew I was, though with the bad
dream and the change of light and waterlevel and this
happening the scene had indeed a disturbing dreamlike
unreality, like a scene reversed in a mirror.

His whole long body began to flap in the water.
He looked so thin and ill-nourished—it would be a
mercy to let the waves take him. It was like consigning

an ill thing, with little life left, to the waves . . . far easier for him, my idling mind said, far easier for all of us.

But would the water go much higher? Anyone fully alert would have seen where the tidal ring lay. But I was not alert. I happened, I just happened to be observing at the lulling speed at which a sad and lonely ballad might be sung, this slow killing of a man I did not even hate . . . and my brain had time and to spare to circle and repeat that strange coincidence, that these islanders were called Turks and Marie was half-Turkish, and to dream significance into it, that perhaps there never had been any Turkey in her, perhaps her ancestor O'Hara had come from here, and people had muddled this provenance through the years, and now she had been brought back to this far island of her origin to be present at and even to arrange the enormous event of Colin drifting away on the tide—as now at last he was, his whole body lurching and pulled, lifted on the lively rippling water and, like a body rested on a machine that sets off slowly at first, gathering momentum as it goes, dragging a few inches away, then a few more, and more, slowly, quicker.

If he wakes now, he will be saved.

If the water reaches no higher, he may be saved.

If not—it is the law of chance.

The law of chance, the suspicion of destiny, made this a fatal decision which no one could alter and upon which, lying there, I placed a careless fascination, involved as a child with whether a thing would happen or not—I'll eat my sweet when the third bus passes, I'll count a hundred before the lightning comes again! —compelled and held.

He floated clear. His head dropped back into the water. Gathering speed, as if hands dragged at him from beneath, he slid out into the deeper racing water . . . and I was up and yelling and running down the few yards of beach and kicking off my shoes and thrashing up cold spray as I waded in. The sea held my chest back like a rope, I threw myself flat onto the water in a swimming dive—swimming even in those deepening shallows, but still kicking the bottom, never losing the ground which was always a last hope in the race of milling waters sweeping him away from me. I lunged forward and grabbed hold of his white ankle. But it slipped through my fingers, shot forward like a long white bar of soap loose in bathwater.

Had I imagined, up there on the beach, that at the last moment I could get to him? Had it seemed so easy, a few yards run, a few feet into the water? Had I felt all the time that rescue was possible—as one is tempted to risk a sharp blade along the flesh, bring it close to the flesh but at the very last moment withdraw it?

Had my mind, during those terrible seconds, worked at two separate levels? As one may listen to the end of a piece of music, knowing that it is time to leave for an appointment, yet risk it, and hear the music with one part of the mind yet see quite plainly

on another level the route and the hat to be taken
to the appointment—two distinct experiences at the
same time? Had I committed murder by dereliction—
at the same time as imagining I could at the last moment
save him? Had I said to myself: 'He's always lived on
rescue. This, the last rescue, the real one, is the one he
must be denied . . . ?

And his white foot slipped further away, and I
flailed the sea with my reaching hand stretching myself to grasp, never quite touching, finger-ends a racing
inch away—so that I had to leave the last solid ground
and throw myself swimming after him, my clothes
clutching round me like drowned arms, coughing salt
water, water clouding my eyes, but my arms always
reaching, reaching—until at the end of a long, long
second at last my hand did get firmly round his ankle,
and bracing back I let my feet search for a grip on
the earth. And there was none.

My insides leapt, in another long second's dog-
paddle I saw quite clearly the distance from the little
beach, the colour of the water, the size of the waves,
the distant wooded line of Tresco far across flat sea—
and then my toes struck rock, enough to brace against,
and I forced back like a man on a precipice, and
turned, raising my knees high and stamping my feet
down for earth, dragging at the ground, dragging at his
foot behind, until the water was down on my chest and
I could twist to get him alongside and lift his head
clear above the surface.

A rock, a rise of ground. It had been chance, a terrible chance which does not bear thinking of . . . but now Colin came suddenly alive and in waking terror started to beat about with his arms, vomiting and coughing water, his eyes rolled up into blind whites. I knew that I had to hit him and I did, bone of fist hard to his chin, clumsily, half on his mouth, smashing his lip and knocking him straight back to sleep. His head fell forward. He seemed for a moment to stand still in the water, hanging his head in shame. And then I was pulling him out, wading easier and wondering even then—had I hit him with delight? Impossible to even try to remember. All that can be said is that I had done it without a second thought. It was the most natural action of my life.

At the water's edge I picked him up in my arms and climbed the few feet to where Marie was waiting. And I laid him down at her feet.

'Are you all right?' she was crying. 'Are you all right?'

'I'm all right. But he's—'

'Not you,' she said, '*you're* all right.' And she had her hands already at him, one cupping his head, the other frogging an arm up and round. 'I meant is *he* all right?'

'Yes,' I said.

'What'll we do?' she cried.

She looked up—and said more quietly: 'You say, darling. *What?*'

'Get his clothes, give him your coat, get him warm. And run up there to the cottages for help.'

When she had gone I knelt there alone with Colin's muffled body and tried to pump back life into him. As I worked his arms the clothes kept falling apart, leaving parts of him naked to the wind, and the wind was cold now and the sun all gone, so that I kept dropping an arm to cover him up again. I did not even know whether I was doing it the right way—perhaps what I did sucked the water in further? Clockwise, anti-clockwise? As the blood from his broken lip dribbled thin in the wetness and his face sagged so blue, I swore at myself for never bothering to learn these simple first aids any human being should know, alone on an island or alone at the top of an urban flat, and grew frightened and helpless and fearfully hoped it was the alcohol more than the water that kept him under.

All the time I tried to keep down a deep and awful happiness that rose humming inside me. 'Oh *you're* all right,' she had said—which as it came back to me now I knew was not carelessness of me but the most absolute care, absolute careless reliability on me, and the thought of it brought us closer together than any bed had done.

Kneeling and shivering in the evening wind, I the reliable moved his arms about haphazard—until a dark knot of figures appeared on the track above and then a lot of them were scrambling down and lifting him up to get him to the warmth of a house, and Marie put her arm round me half-embracing half-rubbing against the cold and the old salt of a boatman kept mumbling how he'd have been back sooner but for the daffodils, he'd been kept by the daffs.

Much later we got him back to bed in the hotel and a doctor came. The diagnosis was more hangover and shock than drowning, and a sore jaw from me. Rest and warmth were all that he now needed.

Marie asked the doctor whether he could fly the next day. 'It won't kill him,' the doctor said, 'but I'd scarcely advise it.' However, we found out there were 'plane tickets available and booked them for, once again, the three of us. He could hardly be left to travel alone now.

Aspirins and beef-tea, biscuits and a thermometer shining under a bedside lamp, and his head sunk into a soft white pillow—Colin seemed to be still the best off of all of us, apart from a dreadful head. 'Couldn't I have just one long stiff brandy?' he kept saying. And then, over and over again: 'But what happened?'

We told him and in disbelief he shook his head, and then stopped shaking it because it was too painful and simply lay staring at us in wonder. And after a while, he asked it again: 'What *happened?*' We told him again, and told him to rest, and Marie smoothed his pillow and after a while we left him stuffed with sedatives and quietly asleep.

We had the brandy. I was feeling fairly bad by then. But we sat for a long time in the bar for there was much to arrange and to think about and even much, like certain heroics, to laugh down.

'You behaved rather well,' were Marie's words.

'And where should we make for tomorrow,' she asked, 'when we all land at the End? Dartmoor?'

And a lot more like that. But underneath we were jangled and nervous and kept on thinking of all we had to do, which was not in fact much, except to send the borrowed clothes back and pack and ask for a bill in the morning. Under the table she kept a fierce little grip of my hand, all the time, never leaving go, as if the hands were talking the real talk, and all over again it gave me that reliable feeling. Whatever else had gone wrong, we were very close.

Once she said seriously, touching on what we had both avoided: 'Do you think he meant to do it? If he did, would he have forgotten like that?'

I shook my head. 'Wouldn't he have gone somewhere less obvious?' I said. 'It was a bit too obviously near.'

'He might just have given up. Given up quite carelessly.'

'There's that,' I said.

When we went up to bed, I was determined to distract myself, to get away into a book, or what was more absorbing, even work a bit. Anything not to go on thinking about it—and particularly to forget about making love. Above all, I did not want to worry about making love, or about the lack of it. If ever there was a night when the face-cream treatment was justified this was that night. Propped up on the pillows, I began fiddling with a paper and pencil and a bit of a lyric, while she picked up a book and, I suppose, tried to read. We were both too tired to sleep, and the brandy was up to its thrumming tricks.

When you write a lyric, it is not simply a rhyming matter. You must think of the words as being sung, of the tongue and the lips, of whistling 's's and drum-beat 'd's. And of the little up and down tune that words themselves make in ordinary speech. It is not enough cleverly to rhyme 'chrysanthemum' with 'Iolanthe, mum'. All this must be sung and make music itself, and this is one of the chief reasons for much of the inferior moon-June bathos everyone laughs at. I was at the time trying to translate a vapid aria in which the word Liselotte had to be rhymed—it was part of a German operetta—and, as will happen, the most inappropriate rhymes came idling through, 'voce sotter', 'got a motter', 'she's a rotter', and across the room the curtains stirred in the window draught, and for a moment I was back in the sea, and then 'potter', 'blotter', 'knees-are-not-'ers' and an odd sharp itch twitched like a knife through my foot, and I must have grunted, and then Marie's book went down and in the same moment she had turned on her side and put her arms all round me. She said nothing but clung close kissing me—and then for some seconds it was I wearing the cold cream of my Liselotte-ing who could not respond, but then I did, and we made love until candles would have gutted but instead under the steady gaze of an electric bulb, as if in this hard naked light we had found each other now for the first time.

Never, I said to myself afterwards, would I ever again pretend to know what a woman will do next, or why. Reaction? Brandy? Defeat? Moon? The male mind ticked over its favourite motives—and the best or worst of these seemed to be that Colin was asleep under the same roof, there was nothing more to be done about him empillowed and safe, and mother could turn to other things.

Long after, when I had turned out the light, and when we were lying in each other's arms, I felt her fingers picking at the plaster on my torn knuckles.

'That's his teeth,' she said drowsily, 'bit you.'

For an awful second I felt she was really thinking of him through the medium of my own wounded hand. But she said: 'I'll bet you liked doing that,' and I could feel her eyes brightening in the dark.

'There wasn't time to feel much,' I said, and risked whispering, 'alas.'

'How I envy you,' she said, firm and loud. 'It's a thing I've wanted to do more often than I can say.'

And then as we chuckled in the dark and sleepily

yawned, I remember adding, 'Perhaps he's sent to try us.'

'Friend of yours in trouble?' said a man standing by us in the street, as next morning they led Colin away to a waiting car. 'Well, it takes trouble to bring out the friend in us, trouble's sent down to try us.'

The island officer in uniform, the plain clothes man beside him, Colin's back, and the sober daylight on the grey tarred road-surface over which these three retreating figures so casually walked—all looked less like trouble than something worse, something sickening and small and dully common.

I looked round at the man who had spoken. His voice had a west-country throatiness. But he was no wise old salt on a bollard: in his brown tweed suit, pea-green pimple of a cap and glasses, he was more like a man with a theodolite, a man whose business is on street corners.

'Trouble's sent down to try us, yes,' he repeated, doubling the echo of my own words in my ears. I stared away from him. Marie had hold of my arm. She was biting her lips, and frowning at these three retreating figures, as if she were trying to remember something she disliked but could not quite recapture.

'It's not till your friends is in trouble, that they don't bring out the real good feelings in you,' the man went on, 'why if everything went right, who's to feel pity at all? It's a test, I tell you, for the best in us.'

'Yes, yes,' I said, and wondered how soon I could get Marie away. It is difficult to be abruptly rude to such mumbling strangers; but in any case she seemed to want to taste the last of this humiliating moment.

'That's what I have against progress,' the man went on, 'with our everyday lives looked after so. Cotton-wool's comfy, but it's a muffler too. You can't do someone a proper service 'cause it's already been done. We're losing the touch of common goodness, it ain't necessary no more, And now here's your fellow, whatever he's done, bringing up good Christian feelings you wouldn't have known without his trouble, would you? They've held the 'plane for him, I hear.'

It was morning, still before ten o'clock, the sun shining, with smells of early petrol and baking. Sounds were lively and clear, the sun washed the pavements in liaison with the sea: there was a sea-town glitter though you could not see the sea.

'Good Christian feeling,' he repeated from behind his spectacles and tweed.

I said: 'Now really, you must excuse us.'

'Oh don't you go thinking it's only Christian,' he said, chuckling as though caught out in argument, 'though it is Christian nonetheless. All this tommyrot about Christianity being the opposite to Science. That's all my eye and old Betty Martin—old Betty Darwin if you like. Christianity's good biology, boy. The old herd instinct. Lick your partner's wounds. Help for help's sake, and for herd's.'

I pulled Marie away as he went on: 'What's the Devil but a test? He's sent to try us. But I see I'm speaking out of turn . . .'

'We'll still get the mid-morning plane,' Marie said, as we went back past the man polishing brass on the hotel door, 'there's a lot to do back in town.'

'Yes,' I said.

'Legal aid—how do we go about that? The office'll know. And then the Adrians—we must talk to them.'

'They might be able to soften it somehow,' I said. 'Could Otto pretend they'd offered to lend him some of those things?'

We were on the landing. A maid was already changing Colin's room. Sheets bundled on the floor, pillows stripped, windows wide open—soon new sheets and a smoothness as if he had never been there: it was as heartless as a well-swept execution yard.

'Damn!' said Marie suddenly. 'We never even found out how much he took. Or where it's gone to.'

'I saw his wallet. It was bulging. He could have paid for twenty trawlers.'

'That makes it worse?'

'I think so.'

'It's almost professional.'

'Almost?'

She nodded sadly. 'What will he get?' she said. 'Do you know?'

Spirits make for size—she seemed shrunk, all muscles slack, bowed down by it. I wanted to say: Go and put all the paint you've got on your face, go and get a new hat. But please, *please* raise yourself, I can't bear you being down like this. But all I could do was soft-pedal it: 'Oh, a month or two perhaps. Even probation. First offender. It's not so bad, not so uncomfortable—some people welcome the rest.'

She tried to smile. We were walking about and putting things in our bags. 'At least,' she said, 'he hasn't got a job to lose.'

Then she sat down on the bed, among clothes divided into dirty and still clean, and wept. I put my arms round her and felt awful. I stroked her head. What can you do?

'Handcuffs,' she sobbed. 'How *can* you see a friend in those bloody things?'

'But he didn't have handcuffs,' I said.

'It doesn't matter, it's still the same.'

I heard the noise of a 'plane droning up, and put my hand over her ear.

'He wasn't even well,' she sobbed.

'A hangover like that would've been hell anywhere.'

The plane-drone drifted away, he was gone, the sky was empty and a clear morning smiled down on these idle scattered islands in their glittering sea.

It had all happened so quickly. There we sat, the same people in the same room, same sunlight at the same window, same morning, same clock: it was all difficult to believe, like holding a death-letter in the hand.

We might not have known at all. We had slept on

till well after eight. Then the chambermaid had brought in breakfast: 'Did we know our friend had the police in with him, and he was leaving?' I had rushed along —but the officer was already in with him and there was no admittance.

I only had time to see Colin shake his head and smile weakly—he must have been feeling very sore in the head still—and in the police officer's hand those awful yellow-leather Ducksweather shoes. Whether these were important or not I could only guess—in any case the officer seemed quite certain of what he was doing and when I started to say he was ill, Colin shook his head again and the officer said, 'We'll see to that,' and closed the door.

Downstairs the hotel manager apologised for not telling us sooner. He had not thought it worth while to disturb us. And apparently Colin had urged him to keep it from us. There had apparently been quite a to-do late the previous night—the officer busy on one of the other islands, and the manager quietly locking Colin's door, though Colin slept all through.

Then the car had arrived, and with it a plain clothes man flown across from Cornwall. We had seen them all come down the stairs and go off. And that was all.

'Come on,' I said to Marie, 'let's pack. There's a lot to do.'

'Is there?' she said. 'What?'

I proposed to her that evening, in the refreshment

car, black England sliding past the windows, the smell of Brown Windsor drifting in on the draught. It was neither the time nor the place, but it had to be done.

It had been a long day. We had raced for the train, and then settled in for the eight hours run up across the great spread of country to London. Sun sparkled on the mortar-white roofs of Cornwall, the last gulls flew off them like tiles, the enchantment fell behind and our holiday dribbled away its last dregs as we ate two hurriedly bought luncheon baskets—as I remember, Individual Chicken Pies and Fish Fingers, and such otherwise wild words today stared a daylight sobriety from their cartons as we talked round and round what could be done in London for Colin, how to find where he would be, how to help him in the courts. But we could conclude with nothing but hope. The matter was in the air, in the hands of magistrates.

Four months, I thought to myself as Marie began at last to doze, one-two-three-four months in gaol as the train tried to keep the rhythm of its wheels and failed raggedly to my baton-fed ear. Four months away, with visiting days. I'd have to make myself scarce on visiting days.

Perhaps everyone must have a private devil. Perhaps, even if he is not ready-made like Colin, one invents one's own from nothing—hence melancholy, hence boredom? The words of my friend without the theodolite kept recurring: in his obsessive street-mumbler's way, he had spoken something of the truth.

And how had I come out of my testing? Not well. Looking back to the beginning, my charity had always been on the grey side. No help I had ever given him had been willing: I had never been able to see him as incurable: I had never seen truly that perhaps some of us remain responsible because it is easier for us—though dull, nevertheless easier—and it is so very much harder for others. Some things are simply not possible, imperfections simply exist—and that is distasteful to our parcel-loving, perfectionist minds. We can never believe there is a situation without a loophole.

So when I had helped at various times, mine was the kind of charity that insists on the poor behaving thereafter like angels. All I had wanted was to put something right, not to lighten distress. Yet his persistence had to some extent purified me—by now I was well in with his problem. I was a hard nut to crack—but he had finally managed to involve me among his followers.

But there again, poor Colin, was he not after all deceiving himself? Was it to him people listened so willingly—or to his problem? It was the problem. What they wanted most was to put straight a house in disorder. You could say no one gave a fig for Colin. It was the puzzle they liked. Yet, as a kind of unconscious missionary, an impersonal lay figure, he did provide a peg upon which people could hang an improved humanity. Years ago nobody would have bothered with Colin. He would have been written off as a 'waster' and left to look after himself. But now, tamer and less self-righteous, we are more inclined to give him the benefit of the doubt. We do not say he is absolutely wrong, or that his troubles are his own fault at all. They may just be 'fault', as impersonal as ever. One looks, perhaps, for a motive in the make-up of his past—which happened so long ago that it almost ceases to belong to him: it just happens to have a name, Colin's. And if we find a motive—which we dearly love to find—does it really help? And do we pick upon the right, or simply the fashionable motive? Do we only grow to know more and more about less and less? In any case, the result may be described by an older term, 'crying over spilt milk'. That we cry, rather than condemn, is as much as can be said for it. What is, is. And I wouldn't worry too much about *why* Colin is. Colin is. And too many people have talked themselves black in the face to make it any different.

And Devonshire was left behind and the train rocked on into the middle counties, and suddenly I saw that if he went to prison, then for a time, however much regrettable, prison would nevertheless settle the problem, there would be nothing to talk about. From Marie's point of view he would be as settled as if he had been found a flat and a job and kept to it. However distasteful prison was, it did mean that the problem was shelved. It would be a time of relative peace.

But times of peace have their dangers. I saw in the flashing black windows an image of life ahead. I saw the terminal station in London, the wide smoky arc of Paddington echoing a safe dull grinding arrival, a landfall from the West, and a resumption again of the old life in London. I saw the Armitages, and Raoul, and the Adrians, and old Belle. And it was not to be faced. There must be a change. Wildly, I began to want Marie and her millstone, the two of them, whatever the price. Other considerations fell all away. 'For better or for worse' simply had to be changed to 'for better *and* for worse', and be damned to it.

I leaned forward and jolted Marie awake.

She looked weak and clammy, wonderful, as she came out of her sleep.

'Tea,' she groaned.

'Tea be damned. I want a drink,' I said, and dragged her up and along the train to the refreshment car, while she said again, less certainly, 'Tea.' I was suddenly excited, a big black self busy with gold flecks inside me swelling—that old before-Christmas feeling that cannot wait.

Yet I had to wait. She insisted on a look at her face in the lavatory, and I went into the drink-car and sat bursting and racing at a table and ordered two long stiff drinks and a cup of tea in case. The cup of tea slopped flat in the saucer, the golden drink bubbled up bright and glassy. In it, like a drowning man, I saw the cinema of the past. A dozen Maries flashed among the bubbles, as here and there she had been photographed in my memory. I saw her against those socks hanging on the roof-garden line, I saw her standing tweeded against the Pest Bungalow at Cruft's and against that sun-fired palm-house in the snow, and holding my bruised fingers on the Night of the Boys, and naked shouting with anger in the bedroom, and dancing in evening dress, and many many another glimpse, all strangely depicting not her but somebody past and gone, with the one exception of the very first sight of her, in brown silk, sitting in the New Marlven. That seemed as instant as the present moment.

And my mind chattered on. Eileen, I suddenly thought, what do we do with Eileen? Answer: Hope, as usual, for the best. She was young. She would meet someone else. She would forget him. If she did not, then it was a million-to-one chance and inconsiderable.

And the human condition, I bubbled at the bubbles, is not a condition, but a half-measure; so why not settle for it? Most people do. And this surely is what keeps them going? The hell with all long faces.

And then Marie came swaying into the car and sat down with a bump and smiled at the tea and the drink and shrugged and took the drink. And I made my proposal.

It was more like a movement towards her than words, and then a big spring back to wait. The most

I can remember is looking down away from her eyes; it felt boorish and shaming that I should sit there, a witness, while she decided.

But it was over in a second.

'Oh yes,' she said. 'Yes. Of course.'

Her hand reached out to mine and a big nervous laugh came swelling into us and we looked into each other, like two nurses at their pillowed prey, with eyes that stroked and ate.

'Of course,' she said again, and I suppose it had all been settled in her mind long before.

I got up and stumbled round the table to kiss her. I had to lean down over her, and the train rocked, and the table held her wedged, so that we could not go on like this and it was silly but I had to go back and sit down opposite her again, miles away. What could we do but throw back our drinks as if to settle the matter? And look at each other again.

And look and look and look—and, wonderfully, not care anything for anyone else in the carriage.

'My God!' she suddenly said. 'I've just thought!'

'What?'

'This one-twenty we caught . . . there's no other?'

'Only a slow old thing nobody takes.'

She looked at me shyly.

'Even the police?' she said. 'Then Colin's on the same train.'